TRANSITIONS
A COLLECTION OF STORIES, POEMS, SCRIPTS, AND ESSAYS ABOUT COURAGE, RESILIENCE, AND TRANSFORMATION

WOMEN WRITERS GROUP
OF SOUTH BEACH

Transitions:

A collection of stories, poems, scripts, and essays about courage, resilience, and transformation

Women Writers Group of South Beach

© 2021 by Women Writers Group of South Beach

All rights reserved.

No part of this book may be reproduced in any form or by any electronic or mechanical means, including information storage and retrieval systems, without written permission from the author, except for the use of brief quotations in a book review.

Cover Concept — Irene Sperber

ISBN: 978-1-955468-09-1 (Ebook)

ISBN: 978-1-955468-07-7 (Paperback)

"Plus ca change, plus c'est la meme chose." — *Jean-Baptiste Alphonse Karr, French critic, journalist, and novelist.*

"The more things change, the more they remain the same."

CONTENTS

My Husband Is Leaving Me *Marj O'Neill-Butler*	1
Seg Way *Pamela Reingold Mayer*	4
Crossing The Line *Patrice Demers Kaneda*	10
MZ *Terry Tracht*	14
On Second Thought *Terry Tracht*	16
A Lesson for the Bride-to-Be *Barbara Berg*	18
Jigsaws With The In-Laws (An Immigrant Story) *Mandy Urena*	22
Transitions *Dena Stewart*	31
My Body, My Self *Eva Maria Kalman*	38
Stuck, Stuck, Stuck *Dr. Joyce Zaritsky*	41
Porcao *Rosa Santana*	43
She Went to War for Me *Mary Ellen Scherl*	46
I'm that Girl *Mary Ellen Scherl*	48
Once Upon A Mattress *Marilyn Lieberman*	52
Diamonds Are A Girls' Best Friend *Miriam Steinberg*	55
Wanna Be A Royal *Pamela Reingold Mayer*	62
An Epiphany for the New Wife *Barbara Berg*	65

Mark My Words *Terry Tracht*	69
America's Changing, Deranging *Barbara Berg*	72
Decisions for Transitions *Dena Stewart*	74
Going, Going, Gone *Irene Sperber*	76
A Revelation for the New Mother *Barbara Berg*	83
The Benefits Of Aging *Dr. Joyce Zaritsky*	86
Tiny, Secret Notes *Marj O'Neill-Butler*	88
A Home For All Seasons *Patrice Demers Kaneda*	98
Down Dog *Rosa Santana*	101
Love at Last *Terry Tracht*	105
Never Too Old to Yearn *Eva Maria Kalman*	107
The Cold of the Warmth a Childhood Family Tradition *Irene Sperber*	109
The Sexual Journey Of A Fifties Girl *Patrice Demers Kaneda*	111
Harry *Marilyn Lieberman*	115
Handstands *Rosa Santana*	118
Moving On *Terry Tracht*	122
My Lift *Dr. Joyce Zaritsky*	124
Sunrise *Terry Tracht*	128
The Silent Warrior *Rosa Santana*	131

My Mother's One-Night Stand   135
Eva Maria Kalman

An Odd Job Odyssey   138
Mandy Urena

About the Authors   144

MY HUSBAND IS LEAVING ME

MARJ O'NEILL-BUTLER

*M*idlife. I had an instant attraction to him, something I can't describe. I thought, *Who is that?*

I didn't see him again for maybe a year. We met again, both looking for the same job. He invites me for coffee afterward. He gets the job. Time passes, and we're both cast in the same show as husband and wife. Same attraction. We have the occasional coffee or lunch on a break. Cast in another show again. Spend more time together. By the time we are cast in a show the third time, I am smitten, and I know he is as well.

Roadblock: we are both married, so we stay friends.

This is a man who, at age twenty-one, a kid from New Zealand, trains as a jet pilot with the Royal Canadian Air Force. He flies commercially for thirty-five years. After retirement, he takes acting and voiceover classes and works professionally on stage and in film. He turns to writing, and his plays are produced. He even builds his own damn gaming computer.

He never owned a pair of jeans until he retires, but he has a swagger when he walks, as though he's still in uniform. That presence somehow makes me find him in the room—every time.

When it gets to the point where he is nicer to me than my

husband is, I decide I've had enough. My ex isn't physically abusive, but the constant verbal attacks have worn me out. Even my sons understand. I'm smart. I have a master's degree. I work professionally. I'm not some weak sister. I file for divorce. Eight months later, I'm free. The night of my divorce, this man, my friend, leaves his wife and moves in with me.

All very dramatic, I know. And to be honest, I think to myself as he moves in, *What have I done? A glitch, that's all.*

We've been together for twenty-five years, though.

Why this man? He has an aura about him that is open and friendly. He is my rock, a faithful partner who is considerate of me in every way. He's a lover and appreciates any gesture of affection and says thank you as I pat him when I walk by. My heart flutters when I think of him.

A year after he moves in, he asks if I would ever—and this is a direct quote—"deign to fucking marry him."

I ask, "Is that a proposal?"

I think I catch him off guard, because he stammers "Yes," and takes me to Morgenstern's Jewelry and Pawnshop for a ring. We have a beautiful ceremony in our backyard on the dock by the water, happy days traveling the world, working out regularly with a trainer, and many delightful times with family and friends.

My older son, then in his mid-twenties, tells me he learned how to treat a woman by the way my new husband treats me.

Out of nowhere, this healthy eighty-nine-year-old man needs heart-valve surgery, which is followed by a stroke—and a downward slide. A year and a half later, everyday things get hard for him. Time passes as he tries to put on his socks.

He disappears more and more. Without warning, he can't remember how to write an email or transfer money in his online bank account. He's had episodes where he is convinced of something that isn't true. There's a virus on his computer. The television doesn't work. He searches the house at night looking for me while I'm in bed. The other evening, he couldn't figure out how to turn off his computer. I turned away because my face was wet.

Now when he meets people he knows, he goes into performance

mode. He knows enough to try to hide his cognitive losses. Afterward, I'm left with this shell of a man who used to make me laugh with his sardonic wit. His daughter says she saw him slowing down. I guess I was pushing him hard, so I didn't notice his losses until it was impossible not to notice.

He needs a walker. This man, who is six feet tall, is bent over like the letter C and shorter than me. Although he still works out with our trainer three times a week, he can do less and less with weights, balance exercises, and strength bands.

Being trapped in the house over the past year, I have seen this decline firsthand. It should never happen to this smart, loving and clever man who is now like a one-hundred-eighty-pound toddler. He's had a great life, but I'm not ready to let him go. How we handle it from here, I don't know.

SEG WAY

PAMELA REINGOLD MAYER

I have a great life. It's busy, wonderful, and exciting. My calendar is gloriously filled with theater, symphonies, movies, five-star restaurants, friends, acquaintances, and happy hours from Ft. Lauderdale to Key West. Traveling monthly Grammie Pammie from Miami to see my children and grandchildren. Adoring flight attendants smile and say hello. The pilots show their recognition with a nod. I'm a regular on this flight.

"I do love a man in a uniform." I smile at the pilot as I exit the plane.

My trips to Europe, cruises, and adventures in Asia are all booked, and I'm ready. I have so many plans, a collage of journeys still to go. I'm a people person who thrives on human contact. Meeting, talking, listening, and sharing are the lifeblood of someone like me. I can converse with a houseplant or a UPS delivery person and be the best of friends in minutes.

Suddenly, in February 2020, it all came to a screeching halt. The brakes are on the world. All continents shut down. Chaos, confusion, and questions without answers. Planes, ships, trains, buses, their schedules are erased, and travel ceases. Live performances are silenced. Now we all cling to purgatory. We wait, we wonder, and we fear for our lives. We distance ourselves from each other. We mask ourselves. Entire populations now look like deer in headlights. Distrust the delivery man, the pharmacist, our family, and friends. One is taking their life in their hands to go to Trader Joe's. We Amazon, Instacart, and attend operas virtually, along with board meetings and telemedicine appointments.

I'm losing my mind. My equilibrium is out of whack. I'm a mess.

"Give me drugs," I cry as I look longingly at the bloodwork technician sitting at my dining room table, drawing blood for my yearly physical. I soothingly utter, "Do you have a local pot dealer? I need a poke of even mediocre hash."

She thinks I'm kidding and laughs.

"I'm as serious as acne on a prom queen," I say, looking her straight in the eye.

"Got to run," she says as she gathers her needles and glass tubes. "Will you be alright?" Then she walks out the door, shaking her head.

I pace back and forth, gazing out the window at the ocean. The pure, no-humidity blue sky is endless as it meets the horizon. I scream out. My voice goes from zero to robust, deep from my chest. The sound could move mountains of emotion. My jaw clenches like an animal ready to pounce on its enemy. I sense my teeth ajar, then the room begins to rumble. My body shudders. "Fuck you, Covid."

There's no response. The fellow condo dwellers roam the halls. The maintenance men, the housekeepers, and the security guards move around throughout the day. Yet I, imprisoned in my own home, pretend to have it all under control. I'm the keeper of secrets on survival. I tease and prod myself on my endurance to solitary confinement—the proud recipient of the Outward Bound killer virus award. I dream and visualize a free world where I can stroll and shop the wide aisles of T.J.Maxx. Just the motion of sliding hangers along the couture runway rack makes me giddy.

Deep inside me, where my soul meets up with my heart, a guttural blast emits from my chest. "When is this shitty virus going to die? Let me out of here. I want to roam the fully stocked lanes of

Whole Foods, go to a Heat basketball game, get dressed up and step out to a Zagat-rated restaurant, touch a menu and relish the luxury of someone waiting on me." I glance out my window and see the sun-worshipping tourists stretched out on the beach. "Hey, assholes, didn't you get the memo on skin cancer?"

No one looks up at my fifteenth-floor perch with my bird's-eye view that takes in life without me.

The blessed vaccine has arrived. "Hallelujah for Pfizer. Praise the Lord for Moderna. I'm ready and willing, but no, I'm not seventy-five years old. Screw me. Screw Mount Sinai Hospital." I sigh.

Every park, stadium, and convention hall sets the age at sixty-five. Oh, not you, Sinai. I'm less than two miles from the hospital, a loyal patient, all my doctors are there, and no shot in the arm for me. Yet, my neighbor Lucy is ninety-nine years old and fits the criteria.

I grab the phone and begin. "Busy, okay. Keep trying." I begin again and again and again. "I'm a bulldog. I'm no quitter. I'm determined, Lucy, you are going to get an appointment if it rips the heart out of AT&T."

After 134 times of trying, I hear the precious ring and a sweet voice. "Mount Sinai. May I help you?"

You bet your sweet ass you can, I think to myself. "Yes, I need an appointment for dear, dear Lucy please."

"Is she seventy-five or older?" the woman asks.

"Absolutely," I say. I give her the name and date of birth. I know the answers to all the questions regarding Lucy, including her bra and shoe size. I let her know that she doesn't get up early, needs a chair, and must be socially distanced since I have not let her out of her apartment in ten months.

"January nineteenth at ten a.m.," she states.

That's about three hours earlier than Lucy ever rises, but who's counting?

"That'll be perfect," I respond and take a deep breath. "Thank you. Bless you. Bye, and stay safe."

I call Lucy. "You have an appointment." Excitedly, I tell her the day and time.

"Oh, on a Tuesday? So early? That's not good," she says softly into the phone.

"It's great!" I shout. "If you ever want to see Walgreens again, you are getting the vaccine on that day at that time," I tell her sternly.

"All right, I'll go," she agrees. "I do love Walgreens. Thank you. Thank you for everything."

Then we say our goodbyes.

Victorious and glowing, I decided to email the COO and the CEO of Mount Sinai to tell them I'm thrilled that I got my Lucy a vaccine date even though I had to push redial so many times, my pointer finger is killing me. I have some suggestions that I want them to implement now: lower the age to seventy and use MyChart to reach out to the geriatric patients who keep the coffers of the hospital enriched with their Medicare reimbursements. "You jerks, letting people who have never been to Miami Dade County, much less Miami Beach, butt into the line in front of your people. Have you no allegiance to your loyalists?"

I also let them know that I did get an appointment at Jackson Memorial North, a mere forty-mile round trip from Miami Beach, at 7:15 a.m. I'll have to leave my Collins Avenue condo at six in the morning, when Mount Sinai is minutes from my door. I push Send and feel better for getting that crap off my chest, vindicated for sure.

I walk over to my sliding doors, step out onto the balcony, and view the pool deck below. "Ahhh," I gasp. "Business as usual."

The thong bathing attire flatters the twenty-something behinds. The European men in their Speedos make me gag. The glistening of the rich suntan lotions reflect the packed crowd in the glass doors like a mirror as they stretch out, mask-less, on this beautiful day. Lean bodies torment me as they sip their drinks from containers made of coconuts, each with a straw and colorful paper umbrella sticking out.

Sure, I'm jealous. Tight-lipped, I utter, "When will crepey skin be in vogue? Let cellulite be desirable so everyone will want some?

Will this ever happen in my lifetime?" Silence. Nothing. I'm on my own. "Time will catch up with you too," I yell down in envious rage.

The beach is covered in a crazy pattern of chaises and umbrellas as the tourists bake in the hot rays. Obviously, they don't understand the science of how ninety-degree temperatures, the sun, and baby oil are a recipe for skin cancer, and in their seventies, they're sure to win a bonus trip to the Mohs surgeon.

I raise my iced coffee and make a toast. "May Covid and the sun spare your youthful misguided thinking and keep you safe to procreate and replace all the poor souls that died from this pandemic that were not as lucky as you damn bastards. Amen." I wishfully thought, *If only I were them and had all that time in front of me. What would I do?* "Screw my brains out?" I laugh. "Oh, boy, do I yearn to be a millennial."

I gaze at myself as I stare at my best friend, my Smart TV, my companion that responds to my every entertainment desire. My reflection shows a woman with a tight, clenched jaw.

"That woman is me," I seethe. "Is this fair? Losing a year of my life to an enemy you can't see, smell, or hear. How do you recapture these missing months?" I take in a deep breath and whisper to the television, "The final indignity that the much-awaited vaccine can react to my facial injections and cause swelling and other issues that require my beauty dermatologist's attention. God save my Restylane fillers. I hope this particular warning regarding this miracle injection is bullshit. I hope I can bear up to all the pressure and pray that my body will suck up every drop of this serum. I thank the heavens above that I haven't heard any bad news regarding Botox."

I've discovered that worldwide plagues bring out the evangelist in me, and I stand tall and begin to pontificate on the glory of a cure and sing out full throttle, "Amen, amen, amen, amen, amen." Ah, Sydney Poitier, he was black and gorgeous before black was beautiful. "I loved him in *Lilies of the Field*. 1963. I, a mere high school freshman." My thoughts drift to my days at Gables High.

The mailbox must be bursting with garbage advertisements and auto warranty specials. I rarely visit the mailroom. Today is the day. I don my mask and grab a pair of gloves. The deadly elevator straight ahead. I push the down button and wait. The doors open, and three good-looking college guys from a possible illegal Airbnb stare out at me.

"Go ahead. I'll wait," I say with a quiver in my voice. The next time the doors open, it's empty, and I rush in and push the lobby button with my elbow then hold my breath. It starts to descend. "Please, oh Lord, do not stop. Let this be a direct trip to the lobby. Crap," I say as it slows and the doors open. "I ride alone," I say, blocking entry.

"Go ahead," replies a young mother with a stroller and a screaming toddler.

"I'm at a bad age. Old," I counter, and the doors close. "I beg you, Elevator Goddess, do not stop."

Then it does on floor number five. A very handsome, buffed boy toy takes a step to enter. I stand in a bold fight-or-flight stance. "I ride alone unless you want to marry me."

He gasps and steps back, and the elevator continues on directly to my destination.

I've got this as I step out, look in all directions, and head toward my mailbox. I feel like Wonder Woman, the conqueror. I have strategically made my way through the gambit of germs, the dangerous jungle of a condo that it is. I insert my key, grab my mail, then make my way back into my chariot, the name Schindler boldly inscribed on the numerical panel. I push fifteen, and liftoff begins to my safe place. I wonder if Covid is in the celestial heavens.

"Yikes, this is genius, pure unadulterated genius." I vow to put my ingenious request out there in an email. I cross my fingers; good vibes ripple through my body. I'm f'ing excited.

I throw open the door, grab a seat at my computer and type: *Dear Elon Musk, I need a window seat on the Crew Dragon vehicle ASAP.* "I sure hope this isn't too pushy." *I can be at the SpaceX launch pad whenever you give me a heads-up.* "Maybe it's time to beg," I wonder. *Please, please, please. I won't take up much room, I'm not a serial killer, and I'm as desperate as a heart attack. Love and Kisses.*

I click Send.

CROSSING THE LINE

PATRICE DEMERS KANEDA

JUNE 1949

The day after my eighth-grade graduation, my family packed up the car and moved from our French-Canadian community in Southbridge, Massachusetts, to Woodstock, Connecticut, where our summer home was to become our permanent residence.

Summers there had been idyllic, full of the scents of strawberries, Mom's berry pies, freshly turned soil, swamps, and roses that flowed over stone walls. My two younger brothers and I would wander all day in the meadows, wade in brooks, and curl up on gently worn rattan furniture to read at the end of the day. Our baby sister was six months old.

An addition had been added to the country house. It had been winterized and modernized with new furnishings that we now call mid-century modern. A fireplace was added in the new living room and also in the game room in the basement. That room had a revolving bar that opened to the cellar, making it quite mysterious for imaginative children.

TRANSITIONS

Our former home, "Grandmère's three decker" as we always called it—even though Pépère lived in it too—because she was the one who had saved money to build it in 1917, was just seven miles away, but it might as well have been a move to a foreign country.

Woodstock was a town of big houses, farms, dirt roads, one-room schoolhouses, and the Hill that was picture-postcard perfect. It was typical of most New England towns, with a white church with its spire reaching for the clouds… or heaven. Its green, formerly used for communal grazing of cattle, was now lined with walking paths that wove among rhododendron bushes that were over eight feet high. Woodstock Academy, a clapboard building built in 1803, dominated the common from above, where it sat on a knoll. To the west was Roseland Cottage, humbly named for it was a large gothic mansion painted pink, and forever to remain so. It belonged to the Holt family and had hosted several presidents during Independence Day celebrations in years gone by.

Where was Woodstock's downtown? Where was the movie theater? From the time I was in first grade, the town of Southbridge had been my territory. I could walk to school, church, the market, and the little ice cream store, which was also the barbershop where I took my brothers for haircuts. Most important was the Strand Theater! I rarely missed a Saturday matinee for a double feature and a serial. I could spend hours in the public library and daydream as I walked by the mansions that lined Main Street. I could walk to the woolen mills or the American Optical Company to sell chances for the school and to visit my Grandmère, who worked the looms. But Woodstock had no factories, restaurants, grocery stores, or department stores. It had no theater or large public library. No mansions lined Main Street. No Main Street! No one spoke French, and very few people were Catholic. This was where people called Yankees lived. They were Protestants. They were also Republicans.

Dad had been the one to announced that we were moving. And he had designed the addition to the house. Mom and Dad weren't people who talked things over. Dad made decisions, and Mom followed. She didn't even think about whether the decisions would be good for her. She just said, "Dad decided."

Mom was one of the prettiest women in Southbridge, but she was very insecure. When she went to church on Sundays, people looked. She worried that things weren't quite right as she walked down the long aisle. She'd always been fashionable. She'd learned a lot from her flapper aunties. Woodstock was not a place where fashionable counted for anything. A few of the farm women even wore house dresses made from flour sacks and had no curtains over their windows.

The ladies on the Hill in the big eighteenth-century houses wore old serviceable clothes… decaying aristocracy, if you will. We wore hats and gloves to church and even dressed to go shopping on Thursday nights. Mommy wore makeup.

Here in Woodstock, there was no place to go except church suppers, funerals, the grange, ladies aid, and the small one-room libraries that were open just one day a week. The population of the town was around five thousand.

In comparison, Southbridge had a population of over twenty thousand. It had busses that went places. We would often go to Worcester or Springfield to shop at big department stores or go to movies and restaurants. Once a year, Mom and Dad would go to New York City for their anniversary, and we children had joined them a couple of times. People in Woodstock didn't do those things in 1949.

At the end of summer, I entered Woodstock Academy. In spite of being a newcomer, I quickly made friends and enjoyed the freedom it afforded after my years at a strict parochial school. I could sit at any desk, there were no uniforms, and I could select my own courses. It was heavenly. The teachers were appreciative of my academic record. At the expense of art, music, and physical education, I'd received a good education in the basics at Notre Dame Academie Brochu.

Here, I made the honor roll every marking period and was elected to Girls State along with my best friend, Shirley. She was nominated by the Daughters of the American Revolution, but I didn't fit that category. It wasn't hard to be a star, for there were only seventeen students in my class.

Yes, there were a few surprises at the Academy. For instance, we recited the Lord's Prayer in homeroom at the start of every day, and it included the final lines, "For thine is the kingdom and the power and the glory forever and ever. Amen."

"Whoa, Nellie!" I couldn't say that. We Catholics didn't say that. I protested and was told I could just bow my head and be silent for that part.

Then there was Charlie, the janitor. One afternoon after school, while I was working on something for the student council, he interrupted me to talk about how horrible the Pope was and related a list of crimes the Pope had committed. Didn't he know that for me, Protestants were the enemy? When he went into the supply room to put away his broom, I swiftly locked the door. He pounded on it until I said, "Okay, I'll open it, but no more talking about the Pope."

However, there was more to our story, as I later learned. My brothers, ages ten and eight, had a much more difficult time. They attended a one-room schoolhouse while the new school was under construction. Both of them remembered being treated harshly by the more provincial local teachers who, it seemed, had preconceived opinions about little French-Canadian boys. After all, they were Catholic and spoke French.

Our grandfathers hadn't arrived on Ellis Island. They'd crossed the line on horseback, in wagons, on foot, and by train from Quebec, and they were here to stay. There would be more lines to cross.

MZ

TERRY TRACHT

I thought this is the way it would always be:
sharing, caring, you and me.
The weekends were always loaded with fun:
a marathon of movies, laughter, soaking up the poolside sun.
But then one day a crate came from overseas,
parts of the motorcycle you ordered, a German MZ.

For days, you painstakingly assembled it.
Screw by screw. Bit by bit.
You hardly had time to speak to me.
And that was the beginning of what was to be.

On the day you twisted in the last bolt, you beamed with pride.
You said, "See you in a few hours, honey. I'm taking her for a ride."

The bikers at the 441 Cycle Shop became your new friends.
And you went riding with them
almost every weekend.

And so, I felt very much alone.
As you, my new husband, were hardly ever home.

I was once so fulfilled with us as two.
But now we are three:
you, me and that damned MZ.

ON SECOND THOUGHT

TERRY TRACHT

It came with a cushy passenger seat,
and special pegs on which to put my feet.
It was cherry red, shiny and new,
and you wanted me to ride with you.
You bought me a silver motorcycle suit,
which made me look fat,
but you said it looked cute.
You got me a silver helmet, too,
so I'd match, sitting in back of you.
I just don't like to breathe in the helmet's stale air.
I don't like the way that it mats down my hair.
I would never ride on I95.
We'd be lucky to get off it alive.
You tried to convince me with all of your might,
and you could not get me to hop on that bike.
In your black leather gear you looked so sleek,
getting ready for Daytona Bike Week.
But when I think about it,
watching bike races may not be so bad.

TRANSITIONS

It could be the best time I ever had.
Unless I try it, I'll never know.
So ask me to come, and I will go!

A LESSON FOR THE BRIDE-TO-BE

BARBARA BERG

I was twenty-two years old, and I was getting married. I was relishing the idea of shopping for my wedding gown. After all, I'd spent my childhood and most of my adolescence shopping in the chubby and plus sizes. Then, when I was seventeen, I finally dropped fifty pounds and could fit into a size ten. So shopping for a size ten wedding dress was a huge deal indeed.

That's why, when I heard that Abraham & Strauss, a department store in downtown Brooklyn, had a bridal show, I was determined to go to it and made plans to go with my mother, my future mother-in-law, Elka Berg, and my future sister-in-law, Sheila Stein. Since Mom and I worked in Manhattan, we picked up my mother-in-law, who lived on the Lower East Side. Sheila lived in Brooklyn, so she met us at A&S.

The bridal show featured dozens of beautiful models showcasing various styles of wedding gowns, as well as bridesmaid dresses and ensembles for the mother of the bride. I was mesmerized by each beautiful model as she strolled onstage, one gown more exquisite than the previous one, and imagined myself walking down the aisle in one of these creations on my wedding day. Finally, when the curtain came down, we said goodnight to Sheila and piled into

Mom's car to head back to the Lower East Side to drop off my future mother-in-law.

As my mother drove into Manhattan, I gave a running commentary on the parade of bridal fashions we saw at A&S. We had just about arrived at my in-laws' apartment building when a car came zooming from the left and careened into the passenger side of our car, pushing it into the adjacent lane. Mom turned white. "Are you alright?" she asked, trying to maintain some semblance of calm. I was stunned but not hurt. We turned to my mother-in-law in the back seat. She reassured us that she wasn't hurt. Grateful that no one was hurt, just shaken up, Mom pulled over. The driver of the other car parked behind us. As they exchanged licenses and insurance, we got out and checked out the car. It was badly damaged and couldn't be driven any further, so I found a phone booth and called Allen, my fiancé, to pick us up.

Ten minutes later, Allen arrived. "Holy smokes! What happened? Are you hurt? How did this happen?"

I tried to reassure him, "We're all okay. Obviously, we had an accident. Can you please just take your mother home? I'll stay with my Mom."

My mother overheard our conversation and insisted I go with Allen while she waited for the tow truck. Allen promised we would be back in about fifteen minutes, so I agreed to go with him and his mom.

When we got to my in-laws' apartment, I got a real glimpse into the difference between our families' perspectives on car accidents... among other things.

We walked into his parents' apartment. My father-in-law was watching the news on TV. He asked what had happened. When Allen told him about the accident, he turned to my mother-in-law and judged her guilty. "It's your fault," he said in a confident tone that brooked no argument—judge, jury, executioner.

I stared at my future father-in-law in shock. How on earth it could possibly be her fault when my mother was driving, and my mother-in-law was an innocent passenger in the back seat. It wasn't up to me to question my father-in-law, so I looked at Allen, thinking he would say something to defend his mom. But he seemed to take his father's pronouncement in stride, and my mother-in-law just shrugged it off even when her husband went on to say with irrefutable logic, "If they didn't have to drive you home, they wouldn't have been at that intersection, and the accident wouldn't have happened."

When Allen and I left the apartment and returned to the scene of the accident. Now that we were alone at last, Allen finally had a chance to get more details about the accident. When I told him what happened, he asked me how my Dad would react.

I said. "Well first, he'll ask what happened. Mom will tell him there was a car accident. He'll ask, 'Is everyone all right?' Mom will tell him, 'We're all fine.' He'll say, 'Thank G-d.' Then he'll ask about the car, and Mom will tell him, 'It's damaged and was towed to the garage.' Dad will say, 'Thank G-d no one was hurt,' and take the information about the car and that will be that."

My fiancé looked at me as if I had ten heads. "No way! There's no way your father will take this as calmly as you say."

By then, we had reached the scene of the accident and found mom waiting to be picked up. We drove on to my house in Flatbush with Allen contemplating my incredible scenario.

Sure enough, when we got home, my father asked, "What happened?"

My mother replied, "We had a car accident."

Dad responded, "Is everyone all right?"

Mom sighed, "Yes, but the car is damaged, so Allen had to drive us home."

Dad gave Mom a hug and said, "Thank G-d everyone's OK. Where's the car?"

Mom explained. "In a garage. It will be fixed in about a week. Here's the information."

And that was it, no shouting, no hysterics, no drama. When we were alone again, Allen said, "Your family is like Father Knows Best. – and you're Kathy!"

And I said – "And your home is crazy. How can your Dad accuse your Mom when she wasn't even driving!"

That's how we both realized how different our families are. We got married anyway. Trust me, our home wasn't Father Knows Best, and Allen occasionally went nuts over some situation or other. Still, somehow, we managed to weather the storms, celebrate the joys and share the mundane day-to-day routines of married life for over forty-nine years.

Of course, the first time I had a car accident, the very first words out of my mouth to my husband, who is, after all, his father's son, were...

"It wasn't my fault."

JIGSAWS WITH THE IN-LAWS (AN IMMIGRANT STORY)

MANDY URENA

Thinking it would be a wonderful way to spend quality time with my in-laws visiting from New York, I purchased a jigsaw puzzle—a five-hundred piece, colorful Central Park scene with its iconic bridge, lily ponds, and brightly colored trees and flowers. We would all sit around my circular dining room table, drinking tea and dunking cookies as we put the pieces together. It would be fun.

Except, it didn't quite turn out quite the way I had planned.

My seventy-six-year-old Dominican in-laws didn't know how to do a jigsaw; puzzles were a brand-new concept for them. I had to teach them to put the edge pieces together first to make the frame and then work on the inside. But my father-in-law fixated on the bright-red flowers, forcing together pieces that clearly did not fit. What was he doing? It baffled me that doing puzzles wasn't second nature to them as it was for me growing up in England, until my husband enlightened me. My mother-in-law, Ramona, had been raised on a farm in the mountains in the Dominican Republic and hadn't gone to school until her eleventh birthday because there was work to do and animals to feed.

"In her world," he said, "spending an afternoon doing jigsaws would have been considered a waste of time."

I wanted to know her story. As we put together the pieces of the iconic Gapstow Bridge on Sixty-Second Street, she put together the pieces of her own life—a simple life of a farm girl from the countryside who'd transitioned into a city girl living in the Big Apple.

My mother-in-law described herself as a very skinny child, dark-skinned with wild kinky hair, which she had to tame with Vaseline. The fifth of eight children and born to poor parents, she'd been raised by her grandparents in a tiny village of Loma Quemada. At eight years old, she was put to work on the farm and responsible for daily chores.

"What was your house like?" I asked.

"Very small. Have one living room and one bedroom," she answered in her broken English. "No floor, only adobe clay, and we no have electricity. Only gas lamp. But sometimes we no have gas because no money." This made her laugh.

"How many people lived at the farm?" I asked.

"My grandmother, grandfather, my two aunts, my uncle, and my great grandmother."

"In two rooms?"

"*Sí.*"

"How old was your great-grandmother?"

"Mama Martina, nearly one hundred year. She sitting and smoking on the porch, but she working, too, collecting eggs from her chicken. She die at one hundred ten—" She stopped mid-conversation and clapped her hands. She had successfully put together two pieces. As she scanned the rest of the pieces on the table, she continued.

She would wake up every day at six o'clock, with the sun, and don one of her six dresses. Her first chore of the day was to take the eight cows to the river to drink then bring one back to the farmhouse for her grandmother to milk. She knew which cow was best by the size of her udders. She would lead the cows by flogging their behinds—not with a leather whip, but a handmade substitute made from the stringy leaves of the guano tree. She would take the sun-dried leaves, twist them into a rope and tie them to a stick. And with this stick, an eight-year-old girl whipped eight large cows into shape.

Ramona's next job was to find one of the donkeys who were roaming free on four hundred acres of land. That could take a while. First, she would call out loud for them to come, but when her cries fell on deaf, stubborn ears, she had to set off barefoot into the lush green hills for an untimely game of chase—untimely because she had to finish her chores.

"Why were you barefoot?" I asked.

"I have my sandal only for the church," she replied. "I no use nothing for shoes."

Having finally caught and mounted her donkey, a shoeless Ramona would ride over to the Albanita River two kilometers away over the hilly terrain. On each side of the animal was a barrel tied to the saddle to collect fresh water from the springs at the foot of the mountain. She painstakingly poured the water into the barrels tin cup by tin cup.

The ride home wasn't always a straightforward operation, especially after the rains. The donkey would slip down the muddy slopes, digging in its hooves in an attempt to remain upright. When the donkey toppled over, Ramona had to help it up by supporting the barrel's weight or un-trapping a leg. "*Sube con Dios!*" she would squeal in encouragement: *Go with God!*

"Ramona, you were a skivvy doing all those chores by yourself. Didn't you have any help?"

"My grandpa and my uncle, they take care of the vegetable field—the plantain, sweet potato, sugar cane, and tobacco. Very hard work. But my grandmother, Mama Negra, she help too," she explained.

"*Mama Negra?* Doesn't that mean 'black mother'?" I asked.

"Yes, she have very, very dark face," she replied matter-of-factly.

"What did you do for fun as a child?" I asked.

"I play with my cousins on Sunday after church. We play hide-

and-seek in the backyard and play with homemade balls of cloth and make dollhouse with adobe."

I listened intently to my mother-in-law as we completed the outside of the jigsaw puzzle. We were finally getting somewhere, no thanks to my father-in-law, who had completely lost interest in our family pastime and was napping on the couch.

I used to love doing jigsaws with my sister and a bit of help from Dad on a Saturday morning, but there were no lazy Saturday mornings for Ramona. Farm work was seven days a week, and she was also responsible for doing the family's grocery shopping at the local store.

I pictured a small supermarket with glass windows until Ramona described the bodega, a small hut without air-conditioning, and the shop owner standing behind a counter. With coins tied up in a knot in the frill of her cotton dress as a makeshift purse, she would pay for what she needed: two pounds of rice, a pound of coffee beans, two cents of salt in a plastic bag, one-third of a bottle of cooking oil, and two cents' worth of soap. With her groceries tucked safely in the leather satchels, the donkey carried her home along the dirt road.

"Ramona, how old were you at this time?" I asked.

"Maybe seven or nine. Ten? I no remember. Nobody celebrate birthdays in my village, so I never know my age."

"So you didn't do anything special for your birthday?"

"Nothing," she said nonchalantly. "Nobody ever say to me happy birthday."

I wondered about schooling in the Dominican Republic. Surely a seven-, nine-, or ten-year-old should already be in school? Ramona's recollection of her school days was hazy, but she recalled starting her education at about age eleven. Her parents and grandparents, all illiterate themselves, didn't see the point of formal education when there was work in the fields. It was only when President Trujillo passed a law mandating that all children go to school that she made the daily four-kilometer trek barefoot and learned how to read and write. But she only attended classes for four years. Then at the age of fifteen or sixteen, she had to face a life-changing transition.

Her older aunts and uncles were all grown up and married, and Mama Negra, suddenly an empty nester, finally had the freedom to do as she pleased and visit extended family around the island. Ramona had no other choice than to move back with her parents and seven siblings a few kilometers away. Abandoning the familiarity of the farm and the only life she had known since she was six months old was an unwelcome change. She went from feeling needed and loved by her grandparents to a place where she felt like a burden, a stranger who didn't belong. With the opinion that education was wasted on girls, her father forbade his daughter to attend school anymore. Thus, my mother-in-law only ever received a fourth-grade education.

Her father, Herminio, was a cold and angry man. Sickly and unable to work, he took out the frustrations over his misfortunes on his children. He beat not only his sons but his daughters, too. Life became hard. Ramona was expected to cook three meals a day for a family of ten as well as clean the house, wash the muddy clothes down at the river, and even help pick the tobacco to make money for the family. Picking tobacco leaves was a dirty and arduous job typically reserved for the men, and it was also unpaid.

At seventeen years old, with only a basic education, Ramona needed to make money, so her mother taught her basket weaving. She began making cushions for donkey saddles, crafting the material from sun-dried leaves of the guano trees that grew on the farm. She would then sell her wares to the local bodega.

Living at her parents' house, she had no real social life apart from family gatherings and attending church once a month when the priest held Mass. Then, in the summer of 1963, when she was eighteen, Ramona saw a young man named Jacinto from a neighboring village working for her father, picking tobacco in the fields. He caught her eye that day and again at a funeral some months later. At the funeral, they talked, and Jacinto was given permission to visit her at the house on Saturdays and Sundays. This chaperoning continued for about a year, then they got engaged.

As my mother-in-law reminisced, my father-in-law kept interrupting to add details he considered pertinent. "You know how I pay for your mother-in-law engagement ring?"

I raised my eyebrows in anticipation.

"Cutting down trees and making lumps of charcoal," he said with a smile.

Ramona laughed at the memory.

Although they had plans to marry, they had little money, and life at home for Ramona had become unbearable as she suffered her father's temper. Tired of his abuse, she packed a small bag and hitchhiked to the city. With her earnings from her donkey cushions, she had saved enough money to run away to Santiago, where her godfather's family took her in. She earned her keep by cleaning and washing clothes until she found a job taking care of children in the capital city of Santo Domingo, some two hours away. As a nanny, in addition to room and board, she made fifty cents a day, which in the early sixties, was good money, and she was thrilled. To put that into perspective, five cents would buy a pound of beef, and eight cents would buy a pound of rice.

As she worked to save money for her future, Ramona remained in touch with her fiancé, penning love letters that took three weeks to deliver. After six months, a lovesick Jacinto begged her to come back and live with his family in Guama. So, on December 31, 1964, Ramona returned to the countryside and moved into her fiancé's two-bedroom house with his mother, father, and five sisters. It was tight quarters, so Jacinto built a hut in the backyard, where the two slept, and they lived like this for a couple of months. Then an opportunity for a new life knocked on their door—a life in America.

In the sixties, with an abundance of jobs in the States, it was easy to get work papers to immigrate. Jacinto's uncle was already living in New York City and could bring family members over one person at a time. That meant Ramona had to stay home in the Dominican Republic while Jacinto went alone to establish himself and organize papers. He would bring her over as soon as he could.

By the time he left, Ramona had become pregnant.

I knew that my in-laws were devout Catholics, and so I asked the delicate question. "So, you were pregnant and unmarried in the countryside of a very Catholic country. How did you handle that?"

"I still go to the church, but I no take communion. But local *chisme*, gossips, in the village, they say, 'You so dark, you not married, and you have a kid. Jacinto will find a white American woman in New York.' I no pay attention," she explained, flipping her hand. In the arms of Jacinto's loving family, she was happy.

Across the Atlantic Ocean, Jacinto washed dishes in restaurants, worked in a factory, and made more money than he had ever made in his life, sending back a whopping thirty dollars a month to support his new baby. Baby Louis was born at home on November 13, 1965. His grandmother, Abuela Lucia, cut the umbilical cord, and after a year in New York City, his father returned home. Together, the new parents went to the American Embassy to obtain Ramona's passport and permanent US residency papers, and to make it official, they got married.

"What was the wedding like, Ramona?" I asked.

"Very simple. No photo. None of my family come. Just for legal papers. No cake. Nothing special."

I couldn't help thinking how sad it was not to celebrate birthdays or weddings and never have cake.

February 15, 1966, was a date my mother-in-law remembered well. It was the day that she transitioned from a farm girl into an American city girl, the day she came to the United States. As well as having to assimilate into a new culture and language, she also had to adjust to the harsh winters of East Coast weather.

As she stepped off the plane at JFK airport, it was snowing in the city after a record thirty-inch snowfall that had closed all the stores and brought the city to a standstill. Ramona had never seen snow, never worn a coat or gloves, and had to jump over the ice in the street. She had never seen traffic, or even a car. The only vehicle she had ever encountered was the Jeep from Santiago that came weekly to the farms to buy produce. Its presence had caused the villagers to run out of their houses to gawp, shouting, "*Aqui viene la maquina!*" *Here comes the machine.*

Ramona was mesmerized by the skyscrapers in New York. The

highest building in her capital city stood a mere six stories. And the sheer volume of people on the streets frightened and intimidated her. In the mountains, she could walk for miles and be safe because everyone knew her, but in this new city, everyone was a stranger.

Employment was at an all-time high. Factories everywhere posted signs seeking help, and with her official paperwork complete, it was easy to find a job. Ramona's first official job was in the garment industry in a factory on Broadway, making "lady pants." Her work duties included cutting off loose cotton ends, turning the garments inside out, and hanging them on the rack. Later, she was trained to operate the sewing machines.

Transitioning into the workplace was a culture shock—not because of the work itself, but this was the first time in her life that she was submerged in a multicultural society, working alongside South Americas, Jewish people, and Italians. She enjoyed her job, and even though she worked hard, it was nothing compared to farm labor. When her supervisor told her to go on her lunch break, she didn't quite know what to do; no one had ever given her an actual break before. On her first day, she was indoctrinated into the packed-lunch phenomena, which meant bringing leftovers wrapped in aluminum foil that could be heated on the industrial-sized ironing table.

Earning thirty dollars a week, she felt rich. Rent was forty-eight dollars a month for four rooms, and food for one week cost fifteen dollars, when a carton of milk cost twenty-seven cents and a bottle of Coca-Cola was five cents. Her salary meant that she could treat herself for the first time in her life, so she went to get her hair styled at beauty parlors and bought makeup and quality clothes from the Jewish vendors on the fashionable Orchard Street, where four dollars would buy her a sharp dress.

I wondered if she felt like she was walking onto a movie set with all these first experiences. Then I realized she had never actually seen a movie. It wasn't until she visited Jacinto's uncle that she saw a TV, and she thought it was fantastic! It was a small black-and-white box, and programming was only during the day. A Spanish-speaking Ramona would watch soap operas on the two Latin channels, relaxing on a soft couch for the very first time in her life. Free time had been a foreign concept in her homeland and had therefore eluded her until now.

"Ramona, you've had such an interesting life!" I marveled.

She smiled, but I could see she was focused on finding the key piece to complete the horse and carriage in the Central Park scene. The puzzle, shiny and vibrant in the middle of the table, took us three days to complete. And in those three days of reminiscing and storytelling, being immersed in their immigration tale, their love story, their struggle, and their transitions, I got to know my mother-in-law better than ever. And although my father-in-law didn't help at all, he somehow insisted on putting in the last piece triumphantly.

I stood back, proud of our accomplishment. Buying the jigsaw puzzle had been a good idea after all.

For a child who had never celebrated her birthday growing up, we—her family—make a big fuss on January fourth to celebrate this wonderful woman who has worn many hats throughout her almost eight decades of life. Her six children and ten grandchildren crammed into the tiny rent-controlled apartment in the East Village as Jacinto cooks traditional Dominican food.

Ramona: New Yorker, American citizen, wife, mother, grandmother, and matriarch, now celebrates her birthday every year with family, friends, good food, and laughter. And there is always a cake.

TRANSITIONS

DENA STEWART

"Another delay, damn it! The buildings won't be ready for occupancy until June 1960," my mother griped after a phone conversation with the head of the co-op board. Her lip was twitching, and her fingers clenched. I left the room.

It was mid-June 1959. Apparently, we now had almost a year to bide time until my family got the go-ahead to move from our crowded, one-bedroom, five-story walk-up tenement apartment on Henry Street in the Lower Eastside of Manhattan to a spacious three-bedroom, two-bathroom apartment in the newly built Seward Park Cooperative Village on East Broadway.

After a two-week nonstop rant about the insufferable heat and humidity, my mother announced, "We're going to the Catskill Mountains for the rest of the summer! I rented a bungalow at Kaiser's Colony."

As she gathered clothes for herself and my two younger brothers, ages six and four, I packed my own suitcase. I was ten and three-quarters. Into my light blue, faux-leather overnight bag, I neatly folded and placed a few pairs of shorts and some T-shirts, a one-piece tank bathing suit, and a floral-print sleeveless dress, should a dress-up occasion arise. I threw in a sweater and long pants when my mother said it might be cold during the nights. I figured the Mary Jane-style canvas shoes I had on would be sufficient.

"Where are your socks and underwear?" she asked after taking inventory of what I had packed. So, into the side pockets, I stuffed my white cotton panties, ribbed tank top undershirts, and a few pairs of white anklet socks.

She said she would take care of the toiletries and other essential items. This was the first time my family left our familiar home base for a vacation, and I had no idea what to expect.

The morning of our departure, my father filled the trunk of our black 1957 Ford sedan with cartons, suitcases, and bags filled with groceries. The plan was for him to make the ninety-mile drive every Friday after work, spend a relaxing weekend at the bungalow colony, and drive back to the city Sunday evening.

As we pulled out, just before we turned the corner, I looked back at the street. It was lined with familiar five-story redbrick buildings, each with a stoop for the women to sit on and gossip. We knew everyone on the block. The women, mostly housewives, shared recipes while their children played together. My friend Esther lived in the building directly across the street from mine.

On one corner of the street was Bennie's open-air candy stand, where I would spend my nickel allowance on a milk chocolate Nestle's Crunch bar after school each day. Diagonally across was Sidney's Grocery, a small convenience store that sold a limited assortment of essential food group items and household products. Hymie's Fruit Market was in the middle of the block. Once a week, he would pick the ripest fruits and vegetables and place them in a carton, ready for my fussy mother to pick them up. Abie's Kosher butcher shop and Leo's fish market were down the street, one next to the other. "Abie has the best steaks, and Leo the freshest salmon in the entire city," was the consensus of the women who rarely left the neighborhood. And Moishe's Bakery was conveniently next to my building. The aromas from freshly baked challah and cakes permeated the outside air. Best known at the time for the Henry Street Settlement theater and art center, Henry Street was self-contained and Jewish.

I waved to Esther, who had just come out of her building to say goodbye. The two-hour drive was tense. My mother, who didn't have a driver's license, made up for what she didn't have with nonstop directions. My father did his best to ignore her. He went through stop signs, drove the wrong way down one-way streets, and slammed on the brakes just as the light turned red when he hit the corner. When on the highway, he did forty-five miles per hour throughout a fifty-five-mile-per-hour stretch. By the time we reached Kaiser's Colony, my parents weren't talking to one another, my younger brother had peed in his pants, and I felt like throwing up.

I jumped out of the car and inhaled deeply. The air was fresh, the lawn recently mowed. I ran ahead of everyone to Bungalow Number Three. Six identical wood cabins were spread out in a semicircle. Even before we unloaded the car, my parents and brothers joined me to check our summer retreat.

"Wow. This bungalow is bigger than our apartment," I noted, walking from room to room. It had an eat-in kitchen, a living room with a queen-size pull-out sofa bed, and a bedroom with two beds and a cot. The bathroom had a stall shower, but no bathtub. The bedroom was designated for me to share with my two brothers. It was big enough to put up a curtain partition. My mother and father would sleep on the sofa bed. The back window faced thick woods with blackberry bushes.

"If you pick them, I'll bake a pie," my mother remarked, already assigning tasks to keep me busy, even though I had enough homework for that. In September, I would be going into sixth grade with achievement tests at the end of the term to determine if I would be accepted into a rapid-advanced middle school program.

After we settled in as a family, we walked around the property. The grounds consisted of a large patch of grass with picnic tables and benches. Five women were sprawled out on blankets, sunbathing. A bunch of young boys shrieked as they ran after one another in a raucous game of tag. My two brothers fit right in with them.

My mother took the lead and introduced us to the women. Shading their eyes from the glare, in between yelling at the noisy kids to "keep it down and stop running before one of you gets hurt," the women welcomed us and invited my mother to join them. To my father, they added that they expected their husbands to arrive shortly. They had the same men-only-on-weekends arrangement as we did.

"That's the Men's Social Hall. It has tables and folding chairs for you guys to play cards. We stick to mahjong and board games and our daily morning sunbathing routine." Flossie, a hefty bleached blonde in a tube top, pointed to a wood structure with a sign that read, All is Welcome.

Helen, another young mother, directed her comments toward me. "You are one lucky girl! Ira, Kenny, and Steven are your age."

Why she thought I was lucky, I never did find out. Ira, Kenny, and Steven spent all of their time together. They played stickball, punchball, shot hoops, and splashed around in the nearby lake. Or they sang along to "The Battle of New Orleans," "Venus," "Lipstick on Your Collar," and "Smoke Gets in Your Eyes," the top pop songs that played on Steven's transistor radio.

I studied and completed my school workbook, read Nancy Drew mysteries, picked berries, and watched the boys from afar. They pretty much ignored me. Everyone pretty much ignored me. I was lonely and irritable as I counted the days until this summer vacation was over.

Then, the morning of Wednesday, August 12, 1959, I woke with a stomachache and no appetite. When my mother told me to look after my brothers so she could sunbathe in peace, I told her I wished they hadn't been born. She smacked me. I cried. She turned her back on me and joined the other mothers on the lawn. I went for a long aimless walk. The temperature had reached a record high, and the sun was blazing.

By noon, I was doubled over in pain. Somehow, I made it back to the bungalow. My mother was done with her morning tanning session and in the kitchen making tuna sandwiches. She didn't look up as I made my way to the bathroom and slammed the door. That's when I saw it. I screamed. This time, my mother came running.

"What's wrong?" she yelled.

"It happened," I yelled back.

"I knew it. That's why you've been so disagreeable and nasty," she replied.

A few minutes later, she banged on the bathroom door. "Open up. I have something for you."

Through the opening, she slipped me an elastic belt with hooks at each end. Fastened to it was a thick white gauzy pad.

When I came out, she said, "You are now officially a woman," and went back to her task. My brothers were already at the kitchen table, waiting for their lunch to be served.

My role as a budding young lady had begun. The very next day, my mother took me into town to shop. According to her, my cotton ribbed tank top undershirts were no longer appropriate. This was my introduction to an undergarment I, to this day, have not transitioned into with comfort. And for the remaining few weeks of our stay at the bungalow colony, I was sure Ira, Kenny, and Steven were staring at me differently. Finally, we packed the car, this time without bags of groceries, and waved goodbye to summer friends we vowed to meet up with during the year, but in fact, never saw again.

As we drove up to our street, my mother retched. The air smelled of greasy deep-fried codfish. Gone was Moishe's Bakery. In its place was Jose's Cuchifrito Bar. During the two months we'd been away, the neighborhood's transition had begun. And in September, I entered sixth grade and turned eleven. These were hardly milestone events, except, like myself, the girls in my class had also evolved. Previously skinny, Tammy now wore a 34B bra. Unlike us, the boys in our class remained immature. They thought it was funny to sneak up from behind and snap our bra straps.

In retrospect, this was a year filled with changes. Sidney's Grocery became Carlo's Bodega. Hymie's fruit market now sold yuca and plantains. Luis Gomez took over Abie's Kosher butcher shop. Instead of beef liver in the counter display, pork sausages hung in the window. Leo's fish market was now a seafood restaurant. And the famed Henry Street Settlement moved to a larger facility a few blocks away.

"I can't stand the stench," my mother frequently carped, referring to the pervasive aromas of another culture's comfort foods. "And the noise is intolerable," she shouted over the sounds of salsa music blasting from the boom boxes owned by the new kids on the block.

One by one, our old neighbors moved to the suburbs. My friend Esther and her family moved to New Jersey. Henry Street, as I knew it, had transitioned into a Puerto Rican hot spot.

Then, shortly before my twelfth birthday and entry into the rapid advanced middle school program, we made our highly anticipated move north to the Seward Park Cooperative Village. It was called a village, but it was four separate identical twenty-one-story buildings, each with three individual building units connected by a common lobby. Twelve buildings in all, taking up acres of city streets. With seven apartments on each floor, the co-op village housed over seventeen hundred families. Our neighbors were primarily Eastern European middle-class American Jews. Here is where my mother was most comfortable, with neighbors who shared her taste in cuisine.

However, my exposure to other ethnic groups was not limited. Throughout my public high school and college years, I walked west to nearby Chinatown and Little Italy and north to Greenwich Village and Central Park. I went to clubs on the Upper Eastside and restaurants on the Upper Westside of Manhattan. I shopped in Midtown.

As I transitioned into a grown-up adult, I traveled with friends with money earned from my first paying job. One of our trips was to Puerto Rico. At a family-run restaurant in Old San Juan, I devoured *lechon*, with sides of *mofongo* and *arroz y frijoles*. I became hooked on the foods my mother railed against.

After I met Stewart in November of 1972, we went to the Puerto Rican Day parade together. I felt energized by the rhythm of Puerto Rican salsa music and spirited dancing. When I told our friends about my old neighborhood, we decided to pay it a visit. The tenements, from the outside, were as I remembered them, maybe cleaner, thanks to a pressure hose. But Jose's Cuchifrito Bar was now a Burger King. Carlo's Bodega an American coffee shop, and the people out and about were young hippies. It had transitioned again.

What struck me most was Henry Street, a neighborhood that I had not returned to since my family moved away in 1960, was only one crossing and one block south of the Seward Park Co-operative Village.

MY BODY, MY SELF

EVA MARIA KALMAN

I stepped out of the shower into the humid air of the bathroom. As the steam receded and the mirror cleared, I looked at my naked body. To my surprise, I liked my reflection.

This takes me back to the hormone-laden times of puberty, the awkward teenage years, and my constant preoccupation with my ever-changing body. I used to take note of the budding breasts, the slightly expanding hips and imagined what I would look like all grown up. Impatiently, I waited to change from a girl into a "real" woman. During those years, the mirror was the enemy I longed to change into a friend. It disappointed me. I raged against it, as I found fault with every exposed part and feature.

My breasts were too small, my waist not defined enough, my thighs too fat, my ankles too thick, my ears too big. Those were the big sins, and there were plenty of little ones, too. I was a late bloomer, and that worried me.

Why wasn't I menstruating like my girlfriends? Then, one day it came --my first period. Even though I had been expecting it for a long time, the blood scared me. I screamed for my mother. She came into the bathroom, looked at my panties, and said, "Don't worry. You need that to have children," and walked out. No explanation. No reassurance.

"Well, that's just like her. What did I expect?" I thought. Still, I felt stupid, disappointed, angry, and most of all, needy. Really, I should have known there would be no warmth or motherly advice. I bitterly recalled the time I caught my mother looking at me with cold, piercing eyes. Scrutinizing me from head to toe, she announced, "No man will ever want you. You have bad legs, and you're flat-chested." That voice. Did I detect derision or a warning? Whatever it was, it left me shaken and more unsure of myself than ever.

Finally, I celebrated my 20th birthday. No longer a teenager, I was still unhappy with my body. The litany of grievances grew longer with every TV ad, billboard, and magazine picture. Why couldn't I have been taller, thinner, bustier, more graceful, and beautiful like the parade of models shoved in front of my face every day?

I married young and had a baby right away. The responsibilities of motherhood brought other, more important things for me to worry about. Midnight feedings, whooping cough, trips to the grocery store, and the pediatrician. My son had a perfectly shaped head but no hair. Was he going to be bald for the rest of his life? Where is my copy of Dr. Spock? Will my husband be drafted and sent to Vietnam?

As the years passed, I settled into the routine of wife and mother. I had become the suburban housewife who took care of everyone else's needs but her own. I was bored and longed for I didn't know what. I needed to talk about something other than toddlers, and what everyone was making for dinner.

It was the early '70s when I discovered the women's movement. I joined NOW, the National Organization for Women. Betty Freidan and Gloria Steinem became my heroes. I found a little book compiled by the Boston Women's Health Collective called "Our Bodies, Our Selves." What an eye-opener! It talked to me about women's health and sexuality. As I devoured the pages about body image, I began to see how futile the search is for the feminine ideal pushed on us by companies that prey on our insecurities. The more I thought about it, the more comfortable I felt with my own body.

It took many years before I was able to appreciate my mirrored reflection. Had I got better looking with all the years? I'm sure I haven't. I was finally seeing myself with happy, self-confident eyes.

Now, in my mid-seventies, I can finally say that I've been freed from the body burden.

STUCK, STUCK, STUCK

DR. JOYCE ZARITSKY

I'm stuck, stuck, stuck.
What the fuck!
I sit and sit and sit,
Having a fit.
But nothing emerges
From this purged brain.
When will this end?
Is this a mutation?
Or just writer's block?
I know what it is!
It's writer's constipation.
I yearn for writer's diarrhea
Without any fear.
I'm still stuck, stuck, stuck!
What the eternal fuck?
I'm out of luck.
The reason is clear.
It's the virus my dear,
driving me nuts.
I'm in a rut.

Staring at a blank screen
As if it were a protein.
I'm waiting, waiting, waiting
to write the great American novel.
I'm stuck, stuck, stuck.
What the fuck!
Asking when will this pandemic end?
So that I can mend.
I'm tired of Zooming
Of muting and unmuting.
I just want to leave this room,
To fly, travel and roam
Without fear of covid.
And so to conclude,
I'm in a foul mood.
Sick of being stuck, stuck, stuck!

PORCAO

ROSA SANTANA

"She's jinxed," the manager told the server. My sister and I overheard him as she helped me out of the bathroom.

"She's not jinxed! You are irresponsible. If your server had been more careful, there wouldn't have been any melted ice on the floor, and my sister would have never slipped on it. You should be apologizing instead of making stupid comments. You should be ashamed of yourself," my sister insisted.

"I'm in so much pain. Maybe he's right. Maybe I am jinxed. What are the chances of slipping on the floor and falling flat on my back, and then having a huge painting fall on me as I sat down?" I said as I tried to hold back uncontained tears.

"You should go to the hospital to make sure you didn't break anything," my sister urged softly. She reminded me that someone letting ice melt on the floor was irresponsible and had nothing to do with me.

"I'll be okay. I want Christian to enjoy the churrasco. He's going to love the filet mignon and especially the picanha."

Although it was hard to sit, I was distracted by the food and so happy to be surrounded by family. My sister kept commending

Christian on catching my head as I began to fall. Otherwise, I could have cracked my head open on the wet marble floor.

Porcao was a new Brazilian steakhouse in Miami, a subsidiary of the original Brazilian chain. *Porcao* means "big pig" in Portuguese. We certainly felt like big pigs after gorging on all-you-can-eat meats that were brought to the table on a spit fork and sliced onto our plates by servers dressed like gauchos. The servers quickly learned that our table's preference was medium rare, and they kept bringing a variety of top-quality meats, trying to fill us up with sausages, chicken hearts, and cheese breads. Christian quickly learned how to ask for picanha, even imitating the Brazilian accent.

Although everyone at the table kept pressing me to go to the hospital, I decided not to embarrass our family any more. Having fallen right in the middle of the restaurant on our way in, I felt we had already garnered enough attention. The big painting on the wall falling on my head was the cherry on top. "Let's just eat, enjoy our time together, and I'll see how I feel tomorrow."

The next day, I could barely move. As I slowly tried to sit up on the side of my bed, I questioned whether I should have listened to my sister. Moving my legs sent painful electrical currents all over my lower back. My upper back, which had hit the floor first, felt bruised.

The back of my pelvis had been second. My shoulders hurt, my head hurt, and my soul hurt. As I slowly emerged from my bed, each step brought on tears of pain. Hugging my preschool daughters hurt. Every position hurt. He was right. I was jinxed.

I went to see my chiropractor, Miles, who had been fixing my spine for a year after a slip and fall in my building. I knew he could fix my messy spine again. When he saw me, he asked what had happened, and I broke down.

He looked at me and said, "As a yoga teacher, you are a healer. You have already healed before. Your body knows how to heal. Let's get to work."

He adjusted me standing up since I couldn't lie down on the bed this time. The chiropractic adjustments were painful, but the effect was some semblance of relief. I trusted him.

He reminded me to do the yoga "exercises" that had helped me after the first fall. I clung to his words—"You are a healer"—and I got to work. I went back to practicing the postures and modifications that got me out of pain. Slowly, I regained my strength and changed my mindset of being jinxed, to being a healer. My back pain healed, and I opened a yoga studio to help others liberate themselves from feeling jinxed or helpless.

Now I realize how wrong that manager was. I was not jinxed. That fall and subsequent pain was a blessing in disguise. It made me do research on my own body and to discover the possibilities of not being in pain. If a cut can heal, why can't soft tissues? My "curse" became the fuel that has given me the opportunity to teach others how to heal their own back pain. How could anyone possibly be jinxed if deep down, we are all made of the dust of divinity?

SHE WENT TO WAR FOR ME

MARY ELLEN SCHERL

She went to war for me.

She trained her body and her mind
She stood by ready to deploy, engage, destroy.

She went to war for me.

She pinned her hair in a bun
She trimmed her nails and polished her weapons
She wore my scepter on her sleeve.

She went to war for me.

She carried courage into combat
She carried comrades when they fell.

She went to war for me.

She left babies back home
She left fear in her locker

TRANSITIONS

She left limbs on the battlefield
She left this world in a blast.

She went to war for me.

She gave all she had
She gave wholeheartedly
She fought knowing her life depended on it
She fought knowing mine did too.

She went to war for me.

She is a patriot of the highest order
She is Anna, Nora, Maria, Laura and Ashley
She is every woman who ever volunteered to protect me.

I am Democracy.
I am Freedom.

She is my hero.

I'M THAT GIRL

MARY ELLEN SCHERL

I'm that girl who leaves a 27-year marriage believing there must be more to life and love
I'm that girl who throws a dart at the world map to find her next adventure
I'm that girl who lives in a tent in Alaska for four months, where two glaciers converge in my 'backyard'.

I'm that girl who with an open mind tries almost everything once
That girl who kisses on the Bridge of Sighs and tangos on the Rambla
That girl who lands on the tarmac in Israel and kneels to kiss the ground
That girl who bushwhacks deep into the Amazonian jungle passing villages indifferent to time, ant hills as tall as huts, barely clad babies, and untethered dogs.

I'm that girl who feels passionately about our country and no longer takes freedom for granted
That girl whose friendships are almost as old as her days on earth
That girl who adores her children and her man.

I'm that girl who wakes up in the small hours of the morning hoping for a chance to see the meteors dance.

It's an august eighty degrees at 3:15 AM and even hotter in my second-floor bedroom.
The fan on the bureau hums drowning out the ruckus of field critters.
Through the 12-paned window I can see the northeast sky from my pillow where the Perseids Meteor Shower is alleged to be most visible, but the view is not peripheral enough.

I throw on a light robe and softly pad my way down the stairs so as not to wake anyone.
Even pup Stella remains asleep at the foot of my bed, assuming I'm just going to pee or to the fridge.

It's safe here.
The front and back doors are wide open.
The screen doors await a cross breeze that never comes.

Stepping out onto the unlit front porch the thought of predators - biting bugs, a rabid animal or possibly a snake underfoot - unsettles me, but I trap the thought and let it go.

I pause on the ground-level, moss-tufted, landing stone. With my toes I test the grass as though I am testing the temperature of a lake.
It's soft and thick and cool damp with dew. Mmmm.
Recently mowed, the cuttings cling to my feet with each tentative step.

The front of this 1830's homestead faces south.
I make my way 'round back to where the edge of the mowed yard meets the un-mowed field, and where the sky is wide open.

The sliver moon had set around midnight, and though there's a slight haze all along the horizon, the dome is dark and mostly clear.

I stand.
I wait.

A satellite crawls at a snail's pace.
To optimize the possibility of seeing a meteor I tilt my neck back, cupping the weight of my head in my hands.

I stand some more, as motionless as the thick night air.
They say the rate of sightings should be about one per minute.
What do I see?
Nothing.

I'm that girl that tries, that goes the extra mile, endures the extra hour, makes the extra effort, and accepts that failure is inevitably inevitable.

From over my west shoulder in the shrubs behind me, the sound of a little life of unknown origin is too close for comfort. I try to ignore it.

I stand.
I wait.
I watch.
I try not to blink.

Feeling defeated I take a stretch, extend my arms into the air, widen my stance with legs fully engaged and breathe in deeply, feeling solidarity with the earth, connected to the universe, and time itself. Albeit lightyears from Perseus.

I don't know how many days I have left, but at 64
I'm still that girl who wants to squeeze as much as she can out of life.

TRANSITIONS

With neck aching and a few new mosquito bites begging to be scratched, I catch a streak of light out of the corner of my eye.

I'm still that girl who wishes upon a shooting star.

ONCE UPON A MATTRESS

MARILYN LIEBERMAN

When he asked, "Was it good?" I lied and responded by flashing my Carrie Bradshaw smile. Actually, a searing pain had torn through my knee and was now barreling its way along my thigh. Slowly and in between spasms of pain, I was able to wiggle my leg from under him. I propped myself up by pressing down hard on my mattress and searched for my slippers—in truth, old pummeled loafers.

I slept like crap and woke up with the after-sex down-to-the-bone pain. As I waited anxiously for a call back from an orthopedist, the morning sun slid through the narrow spaces of the blinds, warming my cheeks. After a few minutes, probably due to a cancellation or poor patient compliance in the age of the pandemic, I was able to book the first appointment of the day.

Still dressed in my morning sweats, I entered the building. Bored clerks sat behind plexiglass windows, sorting papers. I handed over my medical information, found a chair, and gave myself a strong hug to stop the shaking.

Minutes later, my insurance verified, I was draped in a white crepe paper "robe" and whisked into an x-ray room. Then I walked into an examination room, where my doctor was saying something about arthritis and osteoporosis. At the same time, he was pressing my thigh, alternating between soft and hard strokes, pausing to ask, "Does it hurt?"

I don't know whether the Percodan I had taken two hours before had kicked in, but I dimly heard myself saying, "Best sex I had in a long time."

He was leaning over me, and I could hear him laughing and felt his belly shaking. When I looked up, his glasses were balanced on the tip of his nose. Still in a haze, I heard him mumble something about Advil, extra-strength Tylenol, Prednisone, and all its sisters and brothers. If I wanted, he could prescribe a course of physical therapy, or I was free to try yoga and Pilates. "It's all up to you," he said before he left the room.

Once home, I reached for my emergency box of old-fashioned Mallomars. Soothed and comforted by the marshmallow mush sliding in my mouth, I readied myself to begin an internet search to determine what was causing my pain. I found that each malady had tentacles that reached out to dozens of others. When my eyes were getting tired and the words "It's up to you" had left me feeling helpless, I found the following: "If you have aches and pains, it may be your mattress!"

The American Mattress Association takes its mission seriously. Their website warned that a poor mattress disrupts blood pressure regulation and the cleansing of toxic proteins from the brain. The AMA firmly states, "A mattress should be used for two things, sex and sleep." By far, the former activity, stated in bold print, got the most attention. They cautioned that anyone with a lumpy, lifeless mattress was destined for intimate celebrations similarly be lacking in oomph.

Reading further, I learned that the Sleepest Company offered a mattress that made every day of the year feel like Valentine's Day. Brooklyn Mattress advertised a mattress on which one could hop around with glee. Istikbal, a Turkish company, offered a romance-technology fabric lined with a ticking designed to awaken the senses. The pros at the Women's Health Organization believed "a good mattress can make all the difference when it comes to achieving the

'Yes, Yes, YES!' high." I realized my mind had wandered from aches and pain to more pleasurable pursuits. Being one's own doctor could have its benefits.

In a short time, I learned mattress speak and arrogantly tossed around words such as zoned, latex, motion isolation, and grid systems with assurance. Nearly ready to push the "buy now" button and secure a delivery date, I searched for a familiar brand such as Sealy, Serta, or Stearns and Foster, but these names are a generation behind. I was now involved with Nectar, Purple, Avocado, Wink Bed, and Fig. In addition, I also had to choose a sleep position: back, side, or stomach. I checked all three boxes, wondering if Samantha would care about any of this.

This morning, two over-exercised young men schlepped my old mattress out the door. Transitions could be difficult, and I felt sad when I realized that my toe would never again be caught in the tear of my old mattress. I didn't know if there was a graveyard or resting place for old mattresses. I wanted to believe they were repurposed into raincoats or perhaps airplane seats.

UPS was scheduled to deliver my new mattress in a few hours. I'd chosen a Winkbed mattress, not for its impressive three thousand coils or bounciness, but because it was reliable and the name made me laugh—the two qualities that I appreciated most in my husband. Also, Costco offered a twenty-year warranty. I hoped my doctor would give me the same odds.

DIAMONDS ARE A GIRLS' BEST FRIEND

MIRIAM STEINBERG

Oh, the allure of these sparkly objects! What makes them so magical? Do they remind us of fairy dust twinkling in the wake of a wand's wave? Is it because they are treasures formed deep in the earth millions of years ago?

Ironically, these precious twinkling stars are tough, their inner beauty released by the skill of a master diamond cutter's hand. Diamonds have long been coveted, smuggled, and bartered. They are marketed as "durable" and "everlasting," just as the love all newlyweds pray for. When Allan and I became engaged, I wanted a diamond ring just like all my friends had.

The engagement ring is a symbol of the bond between the groom and his bride, but since Allan's mother insisted on joining us for the shopping excursion, I worried it foretold the future bond between the three of us.

Luckily, having grown to be a young Jewish woman raised to never pay retail for high-ticket items, I was prepared. I had a connection. I had arranged with my old friend from Teen Tour, Alex, to meet with his father, a New York City diamond district magnate.

The three of us wended past a maze of first-floor jewelry stalls, into a high-rise elevator. The door opened onto corridors lined with single gray doors protected by elaborate security systems until we were finally ushered to the inner sanctum. Here diamond deals were made across boxy wooden desks. Alex's dad and uncle sat facing each other, deftly unfolding blue-tinged parcel papers inside which tiny treasures were revealed. They sparkled under jeweler's loupes above which one eye squinted while the other's eyebrow rose as if to question, "Is *this* the one?" Color, brilliance, cut, clarity, and carat, we were schooled.

Alex's dad and uncle did very well by us. My future mother-in-law would have liked a bigger stone, but I was adamant that it had to be within Allan's means. I know. I know. I could have had a much bigger ring, but that was the kind of girl I was in those days.

Decades passed. I was still happy with my one-carat bling, but the setting was crying out for change. Life sometimes seems like a series of coincidences. While I had long before lost touch with Teen Tour Alex, I had become close friends with his cousin Anne when we joined the same book club. Naturally, when I decided to reset that stone, it was Anne and *her* father I called on. We marveled how the diamond had come full circle from the beginning of my marriage to its maturation, from her cousin and her uncle to herself and her father. It was a sweet coincidence.

It seemed an eternity had passed in my forever-and-a-day deliberations before I could decide on a design for the setting, but I was thrilled with the results—a wide matte-platinum band with the oval stone turned horizontally to show it to better advantage. I thought it very elegant and sophisticated. I enjoyed wearing it until I put on some weight and suddenly found my finger had swelled along with the rest of me.

One day, the ring, which slid over my knuckle at the beginning of the evening, was swallowed by rolls of fat beneath my knuckle at the end of the evening. The more I struggled, the more the ring viciously tightened its grasp. I started to envision an ER visit involving electric saws. But after copious amounts of dishwashing soap, freezing water, and pain, the ring twisted off.

There is no excuse for what I did next. I dried it off with a paper towel and left it in the paper towel on the kitchen counter. I was too tired and lazy to climb the stairs and put it away in its box in my jewelry drawer. All I wanted to do was veg out in front of the television for half an hour before collapsing in bed.

"You'd better not leave your ring on the counter like that," Allan chastised me. "I guarantee you it's going to end up being accidentally thrown out." He meant he would throw it out in his never-ending quest to tidy up after me.

So I took the wrapped-up ring and put it in my shoulder bag—aka large cavernous black hole—for safekeeping, until such time that I would no longer be too lazy to climb the stairs and put it away properly.

A few days later, I thought of the ring. I searched my bag carefully, but it wasn't there. I asked Allan if he had seen it. He hadn't, but he helped me search. It wouldn't be the first time he'd found a piece of my jewelry glittering on the bedroom carpet. This time, we had no such luck. More days passed, and a horrifying thought meandered through my mind.

Wait a minute. Didn't I meet a friend for coffee in Starbucks? And wasn't she late? And didn't I spend the time cleaning out my shoulder bag? When was that? After I stowed the ring there for safekeeping? Oh. My. God.

I wish I could tell you that I raced to Starbucks, searched their dumpsters, and found the ring wrapped up in its napkin. Or failing that, because of course it was no longer in the dumpster, I tracked down the sanitation guys and hitched a ride with them to the dump, then we all searched the dunes together until one of us miraculously found it. In my imagination, I hold up the newspaper clipping as proof. But that's not what happened. For reasons I do not understand, I could not envision myself dumpster diving or searching for diamond needles in garbage haystacks, let alone propel myself into action. I never saw my diamond ring again.

When my mother died, after the ordeal of going through the clothing and pockets and dresser drawers, the divvying of her jewelry turned out to be a welcome reprieve.

My sister and I sat cross-legged on Mom's bed with the three-tiered black leather jewelry box between us. The leather was flaking with age; the velvet interior was scuffed and worn with use. But the process of choosing pieces was surprisingly amicable and smooth. Our tastes in jewelry didn't always converge, my sister's, mine, and certainly not my mother's. It saddened me that there weren't many important pieces. The box was bursting with mostly costume and less expensive items. It was a lifetime's collection and not much to show for it.

We sorted everything into piles—costume, gold, pearls, and silver. When we came upon our grandfather's gold pocket watch with the long pendant chain my mother had worn with it, I found it easy to say, "Why don't you take it? You had a close relationship with Zeydeh, and I barely knew him." It had been high on her wish list and she thanked me sincerely.

She liked the long strands of pearls, and I preferred the choker and bracelet.

There was an old gray suede ring box with the Fortunoff's logo stamped across the top. Nestled inside was Mom's diamond ring. Quickly, I said, "I'd like to have this to replace the diamond ring I lost years ago. I'll think of Mom when I wear it." The shame of having lost my ring was still with me. Replacing it with my mother's imbued the loss with meaning.

Now, this wasn't Mom's original diamond engagement ring, because, to the best of my knowledge, she'd never had one. I looked at the few wedding pictures we have, but her hand is hidden by the floral bouquet. It was 1945. There was a war on. They could barely pay for the wedding. She had made her wedding dress. In fact, I think my mom paid for the wedding herself. I feel pride when I think of the responsibilities she shouldered as the only child of struggling immigrant parents. I don't think my dad had an extra cent to buy her a diamond engagement ring. This was more like a fancy cocktail ring with a kind of art deco-like feel that was bought much later.

In fact, my friend Anne told me it dates from the late sixties and early seventies, a round diamond nestled in the spot where the two sides of the loop meet—reminiscent of a musical treble notation. The arms were covered in pavé stones. Not only was the setting not to my taste, but the loop had a way of catching on clothing. I knew I had to reset it. The question, once again, was how.

The ring sat in my drawer for a long time while I tried to decide Something modern that could be worn daily? Something fancier for evenings out? I searched and searched and searched, looking at design after design.

I kept going back to the ring I had redone. Eventually, I saw a ring that was identical to the one I had lost. But this one had pavé stones along the sides of the band. I had found the answer. After all, my mom's ring had pavé stones in the setting, so it was perfect. I could get optimal use out of her ring!

What a relief to have finally made a decision, one that felt so right. Then began the process of having the new ring made. Back and forth Anne and I went with measurements and decisions about materials. White gold or platinum? How far should the tiny pavé stones go around the band?

The jeweler had bad news: "We can't use your mother's pavé stones, they're too small and not the right kind. They won't hold up." Anne now had to get new pavé stones. More checking. More measurements. More back-and-forth. More emailing pictures. The model was finally finished. Anne delivered a blue clay model for me to try on. She unwrapped the diamond from the special parcel paper. "Careful! Don't lose the diamond."

We gingerly placed it in the clay setting to see how the ring would look. The loose diamond tumbled out. I grabbed the setting to steady it and broke the clay model.

In the meantime, I had noticed something was wrong. I didn't like the angle of the shaft. I wanted the plane to lie flatter. More checking. More looking at different angles. More time passed.

The phone rang. It was Anne. My heart jumped. Could the ring finally be ready?

"Listen," she said sheepishly. "I don't know how to tell you this, but I have *bad* news."

Oh shit! Now what? Was the stone stolen? But then they're insured, aren't they? Is it going to take longer than she thought? Okay, I waited this long. I'll wait a little longer.

Prickles crept up my neck as I waited silently for what was coming.

"The jeweler was about to put the stone in the ring," Anne continued cautiously, "when he took a good look, and he noticed that the stone isn't real."

"What!" I yelled. "How is it possible that no one noticed that before? The stone was taken out and measured for the new setting, wasn't it?"

"Did you have any inkling that the stone might not have been real? Do you remember hearing anything about it growing up?" Anne asked.

"Of course not!" I bellowed. "Why would I want to invest all that money into a setting for a fake stone?"

Now I questioned Anne. "What about the people who were holding onto the ring all these months? Could anyone have swapped out the real stone for a fake one?"

But Anne assured me she had complete trust in everyone she worked with.

I didn't know what to do. I felt angry. I felt tricked. But if I had been tricked, who had done the tricking?

There are many people I know, people who would never identify in the *victim* role, who would scream bloody murder, and insist that since no one had said the stone wasn't real until the end, it must be replaced with a real stone. Later, they might retell the story with pride in how they had beaten the system. But I had already trusted Anne many times before. I had always known Anne to be an honest and generous person.

So, despite the weight in my chest and the crawling sensation up the back of my neck and scull, I believed her when she said the stone I had given her was a very good cubic zirconia and that there had been something off about the weight in relation to its size from the beginning.

It wasn't totally shocking that my parents would end up with a cubic zirconia. I wondered if some unscrupulous salesperson or jeweler had swapped out my mother's stone for a fake. Did my father buy the ring and tell her it was a real diamond? Or did my parents decide *together* to buy a very good cubic zirconia because it looked just as good as a real diamond and cost much less? After all, they were the same people who'd tried to pawn off a fake Barbie Dreamhouse on me to save a few bucks one Chanukah.

Anne's voice disrupted my musings. "So, what do you think you want to do?" she asked. "You could forget the whole thing. You could go ahead and set the ring with your mother's stone. No one will be able to tell it's not real unless they examine it with a loupe. Or we can look around for a diamond to fit in its place."

Well, I thought, *the ring is already made.* Maybe they would see if someone else would buy it. But by now, I thought of it as *my* ring. After all the time and effort, I would be left right back where I had started—with no ring.

Again, I felt tricked. I felt someone, perhaps God, was playing a cosmic joke on me. Or maybe my mother was trying to teach me a lesson from the beyond. But what *was* the lesson?

Was it your eyes can be fooled by sparkly things? Spend your money wisely, not on frivolous things? Was she saying: "Why are you always so spoiled? Why aren't you satisfied with what you have?"

I decided to take the situation at face value. The ring is beautiful. The stone was, after all, my mother's, even though it isn't a real diamond. I would not put the stone back in a drawer. I would take it for the cosmic joke and life lesson it was, wear it, and enjoy it. It certainly was a reminder of Mom.

No, I've made far too pretty a conclusion. I've wrapped it all up neatly in a bow. This is *not* a ring to take at face value. This is a ring to make you think. This is a ring to make you *wonder*. About the importance we place on material objects, the meaning we assign to symbols of love, and the point at which memory turns to mystery.

WANNA BE A ROYAL

PAMELA REINGOLD MAYER

*P*oor Meghan. Poor Harry. A hex on you, British press. How dare you, Royal rotten family? So the Prince and Meghan, aka Duke and Duchess of Sussex, had to stay at Tyler Perry's crummy $17,000,000 mansion in the slum neighborhood known as Beverly Ridge Estates in LA, California. They have to put up with old money and mega-rich business types in Perry's hood. Woe is me.

Suddenly, long hours of hitting the pavement finally paid off. Meghan and Harry found their forever home. They're first-time homeowners in the upscale seaside town of Santa Barbara—or is it Montecito? Or are they one and the same? They are quite happy in their very own $14,650,000.22 estate. It's a lovely decadence that includes a two-bedroom guest house for her mom or his grandmother, better known as the Queen, when she comes to visit at Christmas.

The new home is surrounded by McMansions filled with the likes of Oprah Winfrey, Tom Cruise, Ellen DeGeneres, and Katy Perry, with her adorable hubby, Orlando Bloom. Archie's booked for a playdate next Saturday with the Blooms' daughter, Daisy Dove. All will soon be the stuff of *People Magazine* gossip.

The family of three—soon-to-be-four—play hide-and-seek with precious Archie running in and out of the nine bedrooms and sixteen bathrooms. All this takes up eighteen thousand square feet or three-eighths of a football field that makes up their home sweet home. At long last, they have a place to call their very own.

I get it, racist, nasty subjects to the Queen. How dare you? Shame on you. I close my eyes to escape this nightmare and imagine that I have a prince of my very own. I made his royal acquaintance at the bar in the commoners restaurant that goes by the name of Sugarcane. It's a setup by the Honorable Mayor of Miami-Dade County, Daniella Levine Cava. She met him the previous summer in London while viewing the queen's jewels. Mayor Cava thought we would be a perfect match. He, the Prince of the Land of Going Nowhere, had been a widower for two decades. I was his last resort since he was aging out at eighty-eight. He needed to look no further than in my direction—lucky dude of a prince.

"Hey, Princie," I said breathlessly. He looked me up and down. He was checking out my black Lululemon yoga pants and matching T-shirt. "I knew one day I'd meet a Brit. That's why I have on my Fly London shoes." I searched his face for his reaction.

"Fly London, my dear? Lovely," he stated aristocratically.

"Hold on to the barstool. I'm gonna leap up. I sit tall in the saddle. Short legs." I nodded. I held on to the bar and made a ladylike landing. "So, Princie, what's up?" I leaned in real close, inches from his hearing aids.

"What? What did you say?"

"Forget about it. Pleasure to meet you." I smiled. "I've read so much about you in Wikipedia and *World Book Encyclopedia*. You've led a very interesting life." I squeezed his hand.

"Drink?" he asked as he signaled the bartender.

"Sure, Sex on the Beach, please." I smiled pleasantly, fluttering my eyelashes as I looked deeply into his red-rimmed eyes.

"Ow really, my dear, that's probably wishful thinking." He laughed.

"It's a drink made with peach schnapps." I giggled.

He let out a roar of a laugh and squeezed my hand. "You are a funny girl. Would you like to hear a joke?"

"Absolutely."

"This joke reminds me of you, my dear."

"Do tell, darling."

"Fine, my sweet. Once upon a time, there was an eighty-year-old millionaire that becomes engaged to a beautiful twenty-two-year-old model. He goes to his doctor for a checkup a couple of weeks before the wedding date. The doctor looks him over and says, 'Arnold, you seem completely healthy, but I must tell you one thing.'

'What's that, Doc?' asks the millionaire.

'At your age, sex can be dangerous, and you need to watch it, take care. It could be really deadly,' the doctor replies.

Arnold thinks for a minute then says, 'Oh, what the hell—if she dies, she dies.'"

"Hahahaha, My Prince Charming, you make me blush and give me belly laughs at the same time." I wipe the tears from my eyes.

It was that very moment I knew we would be engaged by the next full moon. *I do hope the Archbishop of Canterbury is free to seal the deal by presiding over our nuptials.*

"You are adorable," I whispered into his ear as I put my hand on his knee, and he slid his hand ever so gently into the waistband of my yoga pants. He was full of Royal surprises. "You dirty ole Prince. How do you feel about princess-cut diamonds?" I oozed in a deep, sexy voice.

"I love them." He sighed as my hand inched its way up his thigh. "I'll love a double-digit perfect stone on your ring finger."

"Handsome devil, my prince." I felt like I was young and in love, and I think he did too.

"My precious little Barbie doll, let's get out of here." He winked and slapped his black AMEX card on the bar. "Check, please."

AN EPIPHANY FOR THE NEW WIFE

BARBARA BERG

It was the spring of 1973. We had been married for less than a year.

One Friday, I was off from work and took it as my opportunity to impress my wonderful husband. So I decided to bake my own challah and babka, a loaf-shaped cake made with sweet yeast dough and chocolate or cinnamon layers. I figured he would be thrilled that his new bride could create homemade goodies as appetizing as his mother's.

With these thoughts running through my head, I called my mother-in-law for a recipe and some tips. I'd been baking cakes and cookies since I was twelve years old. That's why I was pretty confident I was up to this challenge. Unfortunately, I had never baked with yeast before and didn't realize it's a whole 'nother kettle of fish (not to mix metaphors). Mom --I called my mother-in-law Mom-- didn't have a recipe written down. It was all in her head. A little of this, a little of that. She also assumed I knew more than I did about baking with yeast--big mistake. *Huge* mistake.

I gathered the flour, eggs, yeast, salt, sugar, and everything else she enumerated on the phone and got to work. I added a little warm

--not hot-- water to the yeast and waited to see bubbles. Once I saw bubbles, the yeast was supposed to be okay. I shrugged, "Okay."

I mixed and kneaded and waited for the dough to rise. Then I braided it. Unfortunately, in my ignorance, I didn't realize that the braids do not have to stick together as the challahs are formed. So I pushed the braids together and ended up with a lumpy little hill. Actually, three lumpy little hills since I prepared three challahs. Uh, oh. My challahs did not resemble the braided creations I was expecting, but I hoped they would taste okay. Surely my new husband would appreciate all my efforts to create homemade challah, no matter how they looked.

I wasn't too proud of the challah, but I hoped I'd have better luck with the babka. I took a deep breath and attacked the dough. I added sugar, oil, and eggs. After rolling it out flat, I knew I was supposed to spread a chocolate or cinnamon mixture on the dough, roll it up and bake it.

The only problem I had was that I didn't know how to make the traditional chocolate filling. With the confidence of a twenty-two-year-old, I pulled out my bottle of U-Bet syrup, normally used to make chocolate milk, and spread a layer of the liquid chocolate on my flat dough, rolled it up, secured the outside edges, and waited for it to rise. Then I put it in the oven, hoping it would be just fine.

Just one more tiny, little glitch. Mom assumed I knew to coat the top of the challah and the babka with egg yolk, so the top would turn into a beautiful, shiny, golden-brown crust.

I put my naked lumpy dough and chocolate syrup-filled loaf in the oven - no egg yolk coating. They sat in the oven for about an hour. No matter how long they baked, how many times I checked, how hard I prayed, my challahs and my babka refused to turn brown. Rather, they resembled my complexion mid-winter - a pasty-looking beige. After an hour, I gave up. I took them out of the oven, hoping they were done. These were not the usual baked goods I got at the bakery, but the big question was, are they edible?

I looked at the challah. I looked at the babka. It was too late to start over, so I placed the challah on the Shabbos table and hid the babka in the pantry. I couldn't taste the challah – I was saving that for the Sabbath meals. But I could try the babka. I held my breath. Cut a slice off the end. A little hard. Not great. But edible. Not bad for a first try. I hoped Allen would be impressed.

I prepared the rest of the Sabbath meals and waited for Allen to come home. Finally, the door opened and my new husband entered. I couldn't wait to show him what I had done.

Since it was his job to pick up the challah, he said, "I'm going to get the challah."

With a big grin on my face, trepidation in my heart, beaming with pride, I stopped him, "Don't bother," I said. "I made challah."

"You made challah?" he asked, doubt written all over his face.

"Yes." And I showed him the challahs.

"They look like globs." Allen laughed. He has no filter.

"I know, but they should taste fine." Looking at the results of my efforts, I understood why he was not impressed by their appearance. But having tasted the babka, I knew my baked goods were edible. Moreover, I was certain that once he tasted them, he would rave about my baking prowess.

"How do you know?" he asked, suspicion etched into his handsome features.

"I made babka too, and I tasted it. It's okay. Don't worry. You can try it."

With that, I placed the babka on the counter and cut the next slice. Unfortunately, the next piece was near the end of the babka, exactly where all the liquidy syrup had congealed. And as I cut into it, I watched in horror as the syrup started to ooze out of the babka. Embarrassed but still hopeful, I looked at Allen for reassurance. It was not to come.

"It's bleeding. You killed it." Allen teased.

"I'll never bake challah or babka for you again." I cried, ran into the bedroom and slammed the door.

And I didn't. Since then, we bought challah every week and once in a while added a chocolate babka to the order.

The bought baked goods were just fine; the local bakeries appreciated our business, and, fortunately, our marriage survived.

I did try to bake babka again occasionally and after forty-seven years of marriage, I finally succeeded! My babka didn't bleed and it actually tasted pretty good.

MARK MY WORDS

TERRY TRACHT

Sam and I first saw each other at a meeting of Brickell Toastmasters Club.

The mission of the Toastmasters was to build self-confidence, communication skills and leadership through impromptu public speaking. It met each week for about an hour, during which we would be asked to speak for one to two minutes on a subject for which we had no advance preparation. Sam and I felt that these skills would be an asset to our private as well as professional lives.

During our first time attending, Sam was asked to give a short speech about global warming. He knew little about it, but he was composed and self-confident when he addressed the group for his two minutes of fame. It did not escape me that he was also good looking: tall, trim, warm hazel eyes and a cute, slightly crooked smile. I found him quite charming. The attraction seemed to be mutual, as following the meeting, Sam asked me to go for a drink with him at the nearby Algonquin Hotel. I accepted his invitation.

The Hotel had an elegant but cozy lounge where many a deal was consummated by area businessmen and attorneys. Time flew over drinks as we discussed everything from politics to art. Sam was a consultant with the firm of Byrnes and Young and he was single, having tragically lost his wife in a car crash ten months prior. He had no children. He admitted that he had not been with a woman since the death of his wife and couldn't even imagine being in a relationship, as his loss was still painfully fresh. He would go to work, come home, eat a take-out dinner and go to bed and begin the next day anew. I had compassion for his loneliness.

I had not dated in months following a bad breakup with a long-time boyfriend. I didn't have much luck with online dating and had pretty much resigned myself to being single and just concentrating on my work as a *guardian ad litem* for the State of Florida. Sam was the first man to spark my interest. We continued to meet for drinks at the Algonquin after our weekly Toastmasters meetings. Drinks eventually turned into dinners and our friendship grew into something more.

About two months after we met, Sam and I went to Le Rivage Restaurant in Coral Gables, where we enjoyed a delicious filet mignon dinner and a few too many glasses of fine French wine. Afterward, he suggested that we get a room in the Algonquin and I agreed.

Sam turned out to be a skilled but gentle lover and he knew just how to please me. He was filled with longing and his desire was insatiable. I could tell that he was a man who had not been with a woman in a while. We made passionate love throughout the night and he caused my body to ache with pleasure. Eventually, I fell asleep in his arms, but my fulfillment was short-lived, as Sam gently woke me because he had to prepare for an important presentation at work the next morning. I had to be in court for an 8:00 a.m. hearing, so it was for the best.

We left the hotel and Sam walked me to my car parked in front of the Toastmasters Club headquarters.

He wrapped his arms around my waist and drew me in like a magnet. He held me tightly, looked into my eyes and admitted, "I think I am falling in love with you." His lips crashed into mine and he kissed me deeply and intensely. My heart was pounding wildly and my knees nearly gave out from under me.

And then I saw it: a Lexus SUV parked across the street, its engine running. A dark-haired woman sat inside. Suddenly, she swung the door open and jumped out of the vehicle in such haste, that she left the engine on and the door ajar. She was on fire and ran across the street screaming at Sam:

"You bastard! This is why you've been coming home late?"

"This is how you treat your wife after twelve years of marriage?"

"This is what you do to our three daughters?"

"And you, you bitch," she snarled at me, "You're nothing but a husband-stealing whore!"

Shivers ran down my spine and a wave of nausea engulfed me. I frantically searched Sam's face for answers, but he did not look at me. Instead, he stood there sheepishly with his head down, staring at his feet.

I blurted out, "He lied to both of us! I had no idea that he was married, let alone the father of three children."

The woman's eyes were crazed with fury. "Stay away from my husband and get out of my sight, you bitch," she hissed at me. She then gave me a forceful shove. I nearly toppled to the sidewalk, but caught myself. I was shaken, but I forgave her anger. I wanted to apologize for the pain I inadvertently had caused her. But when I looked at her tortured face, I turned around and walked away instead.

AMERICA'S CHANGING, DERANGING

BARBARA BERG

Don't be a cop
you'll be abused.
Don't be a doctor
you'll get sued.

A businessman
you'll be defamed.
If you're a lawyer
be ashamed.

If you're rich
you'll be okay.
If you are poor
the state will pay.

But if you're
in the middle class
There's nobody
to save your ass.

Be a crook
you'll be excused.
If you're a victim
you're so screwed.

No one's acting
like they should.
Good is bad
and bad is good.

The strong are weak
The weak are strong.
False is true.
And right is wrong.

Man is woman
Woman man
I don't know who
The hell I am.

But one thing
That I know is true
For him-she, her-he
Me and you.

No matter what
you say or do,
No matter what
your point of view.

No one knows
what lies ahead.
But one day
We will all be dead.

DECISIONS FOR TRANSITIONS

DENA STEWART

Her morning coffee go-with was reading the World News,
then, for fun, her horoscope for futuristic clues.

According to astrology, the weight in all decisions
are not coincidental, but zodiac positions.

Born a full-fledged Libra, she craved a balanced scale.
Thoughtful and intelligent, she didn't like to fail.

So when her Astro "sign" said that her stars were in alignment,
she was able to deliver an improved assignment.

Her weakness was a need for calm when others were explosive.
When harmony was shaken, her insides were corrosive.

This day, her horoscope suggested she would meet her mate.
As destiny would have it, she went on a blind date.

Her type of energy was Air. It drove her social actions.
The man she met, a Capricorn, had contrasting reactions.

Earth was his compelling force. For him, there's no pretending.
Though disciplined, he caused chaos and often was unbending.

Their love was true with certainty, although it wasn't easy
for her to give up balance when the tilt made her feel queasy.

For their relationship to work without major divisions,
they allowed for providence to guide them through transitions.

Both agreed to compromise when one was out of range.
Her dissention honored when he subscribed to change.

This Libra and her Capricorn, together fifty years,
thank the lucky stars for sharing laughter and some tears.

Note: He inspired her to grow and take risks on her own.
And she got him to fold his clothes and leave his comfort zone.

GOING, GOING, GONE

IRENE SPERBER

NEW YORK CITY - AGE 32, EARLY WINTER 1982

"How would you like to go to the Far East with me?" the man I'd been happily "seeing" for a year said to me. He was offered a corporate promotion transfer in Hong Kong, departing in six months. It was his second overseas career assignment to date.

R—we'll call him "R" for a sliver of privacy—levied the question into our dialogue as we sat across from each other, separated by a small dining table overlooking the end-of-day twinkling lights on the Hudson River.

After a nervous smart-alecky remark of "How far east? York Avenue?" I turned my gaze toward the view from his sixteenth-floor Upper West Side apartment. Settling into a deep pause, I asked myself, *What is all this going to mean?*

The tsunami of choices signaled a fork in the road, washing over the future.

R and I decided after many weeks of angst and much back-and-forth that, yes, we would go together, but we would need to get married first. This was a marriage proposal—serious stuff.

Oh. Well. New wrinkle. Forever, huh?

I had been "there" before, as had he, and I needed to consider the implications of giving up my apartment, a job, and all life as I knew it for corporate-expatriate-wife status. Conversely, I could not see tossing this relationship into an ever-moving tide. We had been going inexorably forward for about twelve months now... way past my six-month maximum tolerance over the past few years. His sharp sense of humor and good intellect kept me un-bored.

I felt change a'comin'.

Early Summer 1982

Fast forward to the newly established Mr. and Mrs. S ensconced on an endless, multi-segmented plane ride from John F. Kennedy International Airport to Kai Tak Airport in Kowloon, Hong Kong. A hill-scraping flight approach punctuated our arrival into a new chapter. The paper-thin space loomed between our quickly descending Pan Am plane wheels and multilevel hilltop shacks of one of the most challenging airports for pilots to land at. From my vantage point in window seat 8B, I could count the strips of laundry lines hung on tilted porches.

"If I had long-enough chopsticks, I could stab myself a dumpling dinner," I remarked to my new husband, firmly strapped into seat 8A as we roared down to the short runway ending at the precise edge of Hong Kong Harbour. If I hadn't been so exhausted and jet-lagged, I might've been more concerned for the immediate future.

A company car awaited to take our bleary-eyed, bent-up bodies to a beautiful hotel overlooking Hong Kong Harbour on the Kowloon side of the British Colony. A twenty-minute trip from airport to hotel was full immersion into a new and "sense intense" environment.

Vehicles full of pigs and chickens, horrifyingly and literally stuffed into the backs of ancient open-slat trucks, spewed their odiferous stench into the hot and humid bumper to bumper traffic crawl. The squealing and squawking are still mighty clear in my mind to this day. After learning that "anything with its back to the sun" was considered food, I made a mental note to stay vertical at all times.

Day One
R happily strolled off to the ferry pier to begin his new assignment. I stood alone in our room of the high-rise hotel, in my fluffy white robe. The breakfast cart was placed appropriately for maximum visual "wow" factor at the sliding glass door.
Time to start my new life.
I had access to corporate real estate searches and lawyers and such. *Oh my.* Mostly, I had to identify a neighborhood that would fit into whatever lifestyle this all came with. Back in the day, expatriate corporate life was... "cushy." One was not left out flapping in the breeze alone.

Full disclosure: prior to moving, I had been given a five-day "look-see trip" to Hong Kong with R, making sure I would not sabotage the company by bailing on their shiny new South East Asia manager upon arrival after much planning and expense. Wives either thrived or created family havoc in the expatriate environment. And yes, it was always wives in the 1980s.

After the cramped expense of Manhattan living, I quickly found a suitable apartment. Located on the Kowloon side near the hotel, it was a hop-skip to the quaint Star Ferry heading to the Hong Kong side's central district, where the world moved in huge cacophonous swarms and where R's office was situated.

"This short, *International Herald Tribune*–reading commute is *so* much nicer than the knuckle-gnawing New Jersey Turnpike ordeal from my New York apartment!" R enthused.

Our new complex sat smack-dab on Hong Kong Harbour, looking across the vital watery comings and goings to myriad glistening high-rises of Central, Hong Kong. The bright two-bedroom apartment was number 1044, or *yat ling sei sei* in Cantonese. It was a primo space with a living room that came to a point like a ship's prow.

Over evening cocktails, we oohed and aahed, looking up and down the harbor from our perch. Only a smattering of apartments were left empty in the recently completed gleaming Italian marble New World complex. I wondered why this particularly glorious view would still be available. Much later, I discovered apartment 1044 was tainted because it bore the dreaded number four, which sounds too much like the word "death" in Cantonese. Local residents avoided renting this lovely apartment since there were two fours in the unit number. I asked about this with a building staff member, who lied to me I'm sure, telling me it was okay since four plus four equals eight, which was good. *Yup, um-hm.* He lied to me. Made that one up, I betcha.

Meanwhile, over on Hong Kong side, R had to make sure his new office space had no bad chi— had to hire the feng shui guy to check the configuration in his new rented suite before any staff member would dare to dip a pinky toe in the offices. R wondered how to make this an acceptable line item to send the home office, seeing how this service was not at all inexpensive, but highly necessary in Chinese culture.

R loved his stimulating new job, the exotic travel… but mostly the food. I adapted to Hong Kong life in our apartment of death, welcoming a completely foreign world of strange smells, different people, culture, food, and customs. It took a while to understand a good deal of their ways, however. Most of the local residents were from China's southernmost Canton province. The Cantonese language was tonal, with seven operative tones in all, spoken loudly and with the Asian variety of an old-time Brooklyn accent. One time, in an elevator, I spoke to R at a higher decibel than my usual mellifluous tones to see if anyone would blink… No one noticed.

I learned a smattering of Cantonese to get by at the local outdoor market. Bargaining was key. I hated bargaining but learned to suck in my breath while uttering "Not cheap!" or "Very expensive!" in my—hopefully—correct inflections. If you didn't get the tones right always resulted in saying something embarrassing and, remarkably often, suggested sexual overtones. None of this mattered. I could've lived there for forty years with a flawless accent, but my face would still give me away as a *gweilo*—"foreign devil."

Practicing speaking to locals in Cantonese was problematic. Because Hong Kong had been a British Colony since 1841, our turf in the English-speaking city center area was inhabited by people who, needing the more lucrative gainful employment, were bilingual and fluent. The younger set was insulted if spoken to in Cantonese —such a thing implied they were not educated in Hong Kong's modern city ways. I was carefully rewarded for my rude slip-up by being answered only in English as a rebuke.

The Chinese culture is very ambitious. Hard work is their mantra. It's not so important that this generation get rich, but that their children and grandchildren become educated and thrive. People were more forward-thinking in the long haul. So very different from the hedonistic heyday of the 1980s urban US mindset, where cocaine, flash, and excessive behavior was rewarded with short-term social "cred" and fast-earned money.

R and I had come to Hong Kong as a viable couple. We were both divorced and had found each other long after the other half of our previous relationships had moved on. However, often a new spousal situation is threatening to old friends. Long-term couples, when faced with fresh faces and eye-batting laughter while in the midst of newlyweds can be unsettling and promote some unfortunate bad behavior. Starting anew is the way to go, no ghosts to vanquish on a daily basis.

As we moved through the months, I slowly twigged to the differences and, more importantly, potential flaws in my thinking. The knowledge base I had automatically assumed from my upbringing was ubiquitous to human nature did not translate to a set of rules in this part of Asia.

Appalled to see a lack of basic social skills, I cringed when an older local crowd on the ferry would seal up one nostril and let it fly from the remaining open nostril into murky harbor water. *Eeeuuukkk!* Then I was informed that our Western method of taking out a handkerchief or tissue, honking into it, then returning it to our pockets made the Chinese population retch.

Our spotless selves were, of course, beyond reproach until I learned we stank of butter. I sat back and had to think about that. *Butter? Butter doesn't have a strong smell... does it?* I started to rethink our Western manners in a less positive and not-quite-as-acceptable light. I was slightly self-conscious once I knew I was "stinky," but not about to give up cheese, butter, and ice cream.

I recoiled at shopping in the brutal local outdoor market, picking out a live chicken, for instance, having its throat slit then returning later to retrieve dinner after it had been hung upside down for a bit to drain the blood. I purchased one of these exactly once, but did regularly eat them in restaurants. The poultry had a distinctly odd flavoring, having been fed ground-up fish meal. I felt much more comfortable picking up a Danish raw chicken wrapped tightly in plastic from the Western supermarket refrigerator tray, though I did have to flip it over a few times to identify the breast side. The Danes must not force-stuff their chickens with corn, American-style, to unnaturally plump them until standing was no longer possible. *So much more civilized, yes?* I was clued in to the fact that locals thought buying a chicken that had been interminably sealed in plastic was the epitome of unhealthy eating and a huge turn-off for their fresh-is-best crowd.

By the end of year one, I was rethinking our entire snotty American wonderfulness. Which, by the way, was not considered so wonderful as it turned out. Another personal shocker.

The copious expatriate population in Hong Kong during the eighties was mostly bankers from around the globe in for a two-year stint. It was easy to make friends since we didn't have time in the revolving-door-social-life to be too difficult.

Working in Hong Kong real estate for a time had been hardly worth it for me as there was a liberal batch of educated expatriate wives to hire at a pittance. I also taught English to Japanese businessmen, though I spoke nary a full phrase in Japanese myself. In Japan, they were taught English by rote in school, hence their pronunciation was abysmal. We read together and cleaned up this problem, along with updating to a real conversational cadence and more modern casual terminology.

Employers knew expatriate wives were not hurting for money and offered ridiculously low wages, which we accepted to stave off a sense of stagnation and worthlessness. All us wives had great lives, but they could weigh in a little too precious after a certain amount of time. We all had amahs to keep apartments sparkling, and manicures and pedicures, and silk clothing coming out our eyeballs. Everything was a bargain. We traveled to exotic locales, bought whatever we wanted, and ate in elegant restaurants while clinging to flutes of champagne with freshly groomed hands, armed with dining companions from myriad careers and experiences.

R and I ended up in Asia for a little over five years. As exciting as it was, I was ready to return to the US. After dredging up a new clutch of two-year-assignment friends for the third time, I was tired of reinventing my inner circle.

Almost to our sixth wedding anniversary, we then headed for a two-year overseas stint in the UK. Expatriate life ended for Mr. and Mrs. S in 1990.

I maintained a close, though mostly long-distance relationship with my Hong Kong BFF. After a few more assignments, she'd returned to her own New Zealand home, minus one overseas husband, many moons ago. Our husbands had worked together in Asia. On company trips, Jennifer and I had quickly discovered like-minded quirks and often disappeared into adventures more suitable to our collective temperament rather than board the wives' bus to chaperoned shopping and lunch excursions.

These international interludes spackled over tunnel vision from my original upbringing in small-town New England, an education that will never be erased and will be forever fondly remembered. My only plan in life was to pile up experiences. In that vein, I am fulfilled.

A REVELATION FOR THE NEW MOTHER

BARBARA BERG

"He's so sweet. He's sleeping like an angel. This is the best age!" Spoke the older woman who sat on the park bench next to me.

My two-month-old baby boy, Benjie, was fast asleep in his elegant carriage, a gift from his adoring grandparents. Sure, he slept deeply, peacefully, tranquilly when we were outside in the fresh June sunshine. But my well-meaning bench neighbor should see him at 1:00 a.m., 3:00 a.m., 5:00 a.m., and 7:00 a.m. Wide awake, diaper full, crying his little eyes out. If this is my son's "best age," what have I gotten myself into?

Motherhood looked easy when someone else was the mother.

Some of my friends could pack up their newborn, drive a car, get on a bus or a train, and enjoy dinner at a restaurant. Their babies slept like dolls in the car seat, infant seat, or just about anywhere they plopped them down. Not my baby. He slept in his crib, his carriage, in my bed, or my arms.

I can deal with a lot *if* I get a few hours of sleep. But, without rest, I'm a bitch on wheels.

No one warned me that infants don't sleep through the night. I had no idea they woke up every two hours. It took me an hour to get Benjie to go back to sleep, and I needed at least fifteen minutes to get back to dreamland. You do the math. I got about forty-five minutes of fitful sleep every few hours every night for nine months.

"Put him in his car seat and go for a ride. All babies conk out in the car. The motion lulls them to sleep," my mother had advised.

Not Benjie. My mother didn't believe me until she drove us to the bungalow my husband rented for the summer--a two and a half-hour ride from Forest Hills to the Catskills. Did my baby doze off? Not a chance. He looked out the window, content to watch the world go by. He did finally close his eyes, about five minutes before we arrived.

In 1975, there were no clip-on car seats that could be readily ejected. There was no way I was waking up my son now that he'd finally dozed off. I craved some downtime. Besides, we had to unpack the car. I opened all the windows and doors and kept him in his car seat. The bungalow was all set up by the time Benjie woke up happy and hungry about an hour and a half later.

Don't misunderstand. I love my child. But, like many other new mothers, I had no idea what to do with him. Pregnancy was easy compared to motherhood. If you are lucky enough to have a baby who sleeps on schedule, wakes up about 8:00 a.m., eats every few hours and smiles on cue, it's a breeze. Have a dozen kids. However, if you have a baby who mixes up his or her days and nights, nurses practically around the clock and smiles at everyone but you, then it's not that easy.

I walked around the house holding him, rocking him, singing to him, cuddling him. When he finally fell into a deep sleep, I gently placed him in his crib, face down as all the doctors at that time advised, so he wouldn't choke on his spit-up. I patted his back to make sure he had safely entered dreamland and tiptoed out of the room. The moment I sat down, I could hear him squirming in his crib. Within ten minutes, the squirming would turn into a squeak, then a cry, then a howl that I just could not ignore.

Day by day, the weeks passed. Then the months.

We spent the summer in that bungalow in the Catskill mountains. By then, Benjie was three months old. One of the mothers in another bungalow owned a swing. Not just a swing. A wind-up swing that featured both an infant seat and a bassinet that could safely hold a baby up to four or five months. I knew Benjie would sleep in that bassinet. Peace would reign, and I would regain my sanity. I wanted that swing. I needed that swing. I had to have that swing. Unfortunately, by then, Benjie was close to outgrowing that swing.

Motherhood had turned me, an impulsive, carefree young woman, into an obsessive nutcase. My life revolved around the tiny human being who turned my world upside down.

Poor Benjie. As my oldest child, it fell upon him to educate me on the joys and frustrations of motherhood. By the time his two siblings came along, I was well aware of the tricks of the trade. I kept the lights off when I nursed them during the night. I relaxed into the role that seems natural to many women. Best of all, I got that swing.

I still don't agree with that woman on the park bench who misled me into thinking that the first few months are "the best time." Each stage of a child's development has its ups and downs. Now that I'm a grandmother, every stage is the best. I get to enjoy the babies, toddlers, teenagers, and young adults. Plus, I get a good night's sleep!

THE BENEFITS OF AGING

DR. JOYCE ZARITSKY

*E*very day, I read about the horrors of aging. We seniors can't see as well. We have trouble walking. We fall often and may even die from them. We are prone to at least a dozen and a half diseases. All of this may be true, but I propose that as a senior, we consider the advantages of aging. Is there a silver lining to those of us who have joined this honorable brigade?

Some famous folks have clearly agreed with me. Groucho Marx's perhaps most famous saying was, "Growing old is great—when you consider the alternative." Mark Twain said, "Wrinkles should merely indicate where smiles have been." While Bishop Richard Cumberland said, "It is better to wear out than to rust out."

I couldn't agree more. So what are these advantages?

First, independence. As a friend once said, "I no longer have to worry about pleasing or liking others. I can instead decide if I want to spend time with them. Instead, I ask myself, 'Do I like these people? Do I want to go out to dinner with them? Of course not. My time is too valuable. I'd rather sit home with a good book or film.'"

I waste less time performing tasks just because I "should."

Instead, I can pick and choose carefully what I enjoy doing and if it's worth my time. I no longer feel the need to impress others. Why should I? What could that possibly do for me?

Best of all, I can eat chocolate cake or key lime pie for breakfast if I wish. And a secret I've discovered—it tastes better in the morning.

Despite the fact that I know that I have limited time on this earth, I no longer need to rush. I can take my time doing whatever I wish and thereby enjoy it far more. In a traffic jam? Waiting in line? I used to feel my blood pressure rising with impatience. Now I don't feel pressured and can actually enjoy the time and space to daydream. I look at others rushing around and wonder where they're going. *Probably home to watch tv*, I think.

I read and have always loved reading. I used to force myself to finish books that I didn't really enjoy. Now I allow myself fifty, maybe one hundred, pages, and if convinced that this book or author is not for me or not worth the time or energy, I chuck it. Why bother? There are so many other worthwhile books just waiting for me.

I can make my own hours. Since I don't have to get up to go to work, I can stay up as late as I want. I can freely choose how I want to "spend" my time. I can go to bed or get up when it best suits me. What freedom! I've taken up writing, a very time-consuming task. But now I have the perspective to write about so much more than I could have when I was younger.

What else? Getting old is not for everyone. Betty Davis famously said, "Getting old is not for sissies." I can't deny there is some truth in that. But for those of you who are not sissies, welcome to "seniorhood." There is much that is positive to say for it.

TINY, SECRET NOTES

MARJ O'NEILL-BUTLER

Diane has just stopped by to visit her mother.

Diane: You look nice, Mom.

Mom: I always dress up for your father.

Diane: Mom—

Mom: I know what you're going to say. He's gone. But we don't really know, do we? If I didn't fix myself up, he could be looking down and thinking, "That's not like you, Faye."

Diane: I don't think so, but—

Mom: Or it could be worse. I could be a sloppy mess and turning into a hoarder. Your father would hate that.

Diane: He would.

Mom: It's been a month. We spent all those years as a solid unit. How am I supposed to live now?

Diane: You have friends. You have John and me.

Mom: You don't come home to me every night.

Diane: No.

Mom: And who will rave about my cooking?

Diane: I will. I always do.

Mom: Or tell me I look great for an older woman?

Diane: Dad said that?

Mom: Of course… you know how he joked.

Diane: You didn't take offense?

Mom: I am an older woman, and he was an older man.

Diane: What do you remember most about first meeting him?

Mom: He had an aura around him and such a nice smile. He looked right at you with those sparkling eyes. If I told you I swooned, would you believe me? I mean, I didn't drop my handkerchief or anything. He had such an impact on me. In a way, I did swoon.

Diane: You've never said…

Mom: Things like that are best kept to yourself, so you can enjoy them in your head again and again.

Diane: Everyone liked Dad.

Mom: Especially women. I had to peel off more than one. And he was so nonplussed about it all. Always said I was his "one."

Diane: Did you have sex when you were going out?

Mom: What a thing to ask.

Diane: Did you?

Mom: I wanted to… He didn't. Said we should wait.

Diane: Did you get your way?

Mom: Did I ever!

Diane: A hussy. My own mom. Good for you.

Mom: What am I going to do with all his clothes? He kept every single thing he ever bought. Some of it's so old, it's come back in style.

Diane: It's okay to leave it for a while. I'll help you… when you're ready.

Mom: I want to keep some things. I've been… sleeping in his pajamas.

Diane: Why do I feel I'm in the middle of a romance novel?

Silence.

Mom: This awful… grieving. Why do we go through this? I should be grateful he's no longer in pain.

Diane: That's something.

Mom: But I miss him… I miss his smell around the house. He had the most delightful body smell even after he'd been gone all day. When he'd come home, I'd run to hug him, so I could sniff his neck. Of course, you kids were important to me, and I wanted you very much, but he was… my life.

Diane: Crap. I want that. Have always wanted that. I wish I were that lucky.

Mom: Very few are. We knew that. (Beat) It's not too late for you, though.

Diane: For having kids, it is.

Mom: Lots of women have kids in their forties.

Diane: First, I have to find my dream man. I always thought how lucky we were… John and I. Growing up with you two. So safe. Loving. So positive and supportive about everything we did. But, in an odd way, I think it all backfired. We're both still single. No one we've met could ever live up to you or Dad.

Mom: Lucky us.

Diane: Dad was so worried about you. He knew you depended on him.

Mom: I had my own life.

Diane: I asked him what if you married again? He said whatever was in the bank was yours. That you'd earned it ten times over being his wife.

Mom: Nice. He always says… said the sweetest things.

Diane: Do you know how much is in the investments?

Mom: He showed me everything before he got too sick. I've been running the house… the bills, and everything, ever since.

Diane: Smart. So you're all set then… money wise.

Mom: You'll be happy when I croak, because I'll never be able to spend it all.

Diane: Let's not hurry that.

Mom: It's good, though, since you don't have a husband.

Diane: Rub it in.

Mom: I don't mean to.

Diane: I know. Are you planning to stay in the house?

Mom: Uh oh, here it comes.

Diane: I'm only asking because it's big, and you don't really need all this space.

Mom: But what if I want it? Maybe I'll start taking in boarders—people who need a place to stay.

Diane: Mom…

Mom: Kidding. I've heard all the arguments from friends over the years. Their kids want them to sell out and move to a smaller place. Assisted place. Disrupt their lives for no apparent reason. Why would I do that? I'm sixty-eight and healthy. I know my neighbors. I can walk to the store…the gym. Why would I want to uproot myself? Your father's death has disrupted me enough. This is my nest… the house we dreamt of… after all the moving. Ask me again once I'm feeble.

Diane: And drooling?

Mom: You can buy me bibs for that. I mean, when I get to the point of not taking care of myself.

Diane: Okay, point made.

Silence.

Mom: Oh God… is that…? No, of course not. You see, my mind's going a little crazy. She continues to stare at a little paper.

Diane: What? You're as sane as ever.

Mom: I miss his notes. I'd be doing something and see a little piece of paper sticking out of somewhere.

Diane: I know… love notes.

Mom: You knew?

Diane: For years. When I'd find one, I'd read it and put it back. So you could find it.

Mom: Notes of appreciation. The things he noticed I'd done for him. He understood I'd given up my career to marry him. He never forgot that, especially with all the moves.

Diane: I could write little notes… hide them when I come over.

Mom: Wouldn't be the same, and you know it.

Diane: I know.

Mom looks across the room.

Mom: See the little piece of paper by the table? I swear it's a…

Mom rushes to the table and retrieves a small folded piece of paper. She opens it and stares.

Mom: It's a note from Dad. How did I miss this one… with his funny, squiggly writing. When could he have done that? He was so sick. Could barely walk.

Diane: Maybe he knew he was close to the end. Read it.

Mom: "My dearest Faye…" He always called me that… "You'll find this note after I'm gone. That way, you'll know I'm thinking of you from afar. I've given little notes to lots of people to share with you. When they come over, they'll secretly hide a note in the house for you to find later. That way, I know you won't be alone and you'll continue to hear from me…" (Beat) Did you hide this?

Diane: I did.

Mom: When?

Diane: Today.

Mom: Who else has them?

Diane: Not telling. You'll have to invite people in to find out.

Mom: Is it just family?

Diane: Still not telling. Dad worked this out over his last six months.

Mom: He's always been a fox.

Diane: You'd better start inviting people over. Dad used up two pens.

Mom: I'm not going to throw a party. I don't want all the notes to appear at once. I'll want to savor each one.

Diane: If I didn't love you both so much, I'd probably throw up.

Mom: (Beat) So I guess I have to pull myself together… find a new hobby. I decided last week, I'm going to use you for a new challenge.

Diane: What?

Mom: Search the internet for Dream Man.

Diane: Done that. No luck.

Mom: Are you looking in the right places?

Diane: I have scoured the internet.

Mom: Maybe you need some in-person scouring.

Diane: Like what?

Mom: Go with me to my grieving group. There's quite a few men there.

Diane: I don't want an old fogey.

Mom: There's a couple of younger ones there.

Diane: And I don't want some young widower comparing me to his dead wife. You want me to start making casseroles?

Mom: Couldn't hurt. What could be the worst thing that'll happen? It'll give me something to do. You might meet someone nice. Maybe I'll get some instant grandchildren. Get you settled... finally.

Diane: Why don't you start with John? He's older.

Mom: He can't get pregnant. That has to be a priority.

Diane: You got this all worked out.

Mom: Not quite, but I'm working on it.

Diane: My mother, the matchmaker.

Mom: I have my eye on one in particular. His name is Thomas Pleasant.

Diane: Nice name.

Mom: Look him up. He's the right age, religion, and has a good job.

Diane: Why do I feel I'm being railroaded into this?

Mom: Because times a-wasting! My meeting's on Monday. Get a haircut, wear a dress.

Diane: I'm not sure—

Mom: I showed him your photo last week... and tucked a little note into his pocket. I know it'll do the trick!

Diane: You gave him a tiny, secret note? Oh my God, what did you say?

Mom: I gave him all your stats. Built up how nice you are.

Diane: I feel like a horse at auction.

Mom: The notes worked for Dad, didn't they?

END OF PLAY

A HOME FOR ALL SEASONS

PATRICE DEMERS KANEDA

*A*h, home sweet home, our sanctuary, the place where we shut out the world and lay our heads. Let me tell you about it. Mine has eight bedrooms, seven baths, four kitchens, five laundry rooms, one jacuzzi, a deck, and three balconies—one facing a Great Lake, another facing a spring-fed lake, and one facing our pool and the Atlantic Ocean. It has a long, screened-in porch and a view of the mountains. There is truly no place like home. My husband and I move effortlessly among these rooms though there is time involved, for they are in Asia and North America, in the Midwest and on the East Coast.

From 1991 to the present, I have not stayed in one place longer than three months. Wherever I am is home, specifically *our* home, so I just carry a small bag even when I'm off to the rooms in Japan. Sometimes my husband gets there before me, and we wait together by the carousel for my small carry-on to appear from between the behemoths that most travelers carry internationally. I always check my bag, refusing to be encumbered, for I'm just going home, where everything awaits me.

There have been reasons for all of this. I have family in Connecticut, so I kept my original house that I'd built in 1980. At the time, I was a single parent with two children. The year-long project of designing a home for us was sheer joy, and I did it alone. I go to those rooms for holidays and summer. The post-and-beam cabin was added to be near my mother when she was in a nursing home after having a stroke. She and I found it together on one of our short drives when we would find a scenic picnic spot to enjoy from the car. It happens to be near a lovely spring-fed lake ideal for swimming and kayaking. I hoped it would be an incentive for family and friends to visit her. It never fails to bring memories of mom.

I encouraged my father to stay there rather than drive one hundred miles round trip each day to visit her. He was ninety-four at the time. He never spent a night there.

My husband's work took him to Chicago, where we bought a condo overlooking Lake Michigan, and we often went back to the rooms in Ashiya, Japan, with mountain views from the balconies. But there was a glitch. In 1995, those rooms disappeared with the Great Hanshin Earthquake. We rebuilt in 1997.

Granted, there are lots of repairs and maintenance among those seven toilets and roofs. I do creative renting, with shorter stays and spontaneous arrangements when we're not using various rooms. I've meet lots of nice people that way—visiting professors in Connecticut, couples who weren't sure they wanted to move to the city after retirement and wanted to try a rental for two or three months, and a traveler in Japan who was stranded after a coup in her country. Well, they were mostly nice, and sometimes a little too interesting, such as the young woman who left a three-foot phallus made of plasticine clay in the bathtub or the graduate student who invited twenty of his closest friends to camp out in the backyard for a week. Both episodes happened in the house in Connecticut. The neighbors didn't appreciate the tent city.

Since 2016, we've been downsizing. Deduct three bathrooms, three baths and two laundry rooms, two living rooms, two kitchens, three bedrooms, one Great Lakes View, one balcony, and a mountain view. But wait. I did run across the street when a neighbor put up a For Sale sign for the cottage directly opposite the post-and-beam cottage, and yes, I bought it. Even our cat preferred that spot, for I would see her sunning herself on the picnic table by the lake when I peeked around back to get a better look when the owners were away. We made that cottage so cozy! Sadly, two years ago, it burned to the ground in thirty minutes. But no matter. I spent the pandemic year rebuilding it. That was a good time to be busy.

That purchase added two bathrooms, a kitchen, a living room, a laundry room, a bedroom, and a deck. Now the home reaches from Connecticut to Miami Beach. The transitions are a cinch.

It's more compact, with seven bathrooms, eight bedrooms, five laundry rooms, five kitchens… Oh, I don't know, but stop by some time. Be sure to call.

DOWN DOG

ROSA SANTANA

My dog saved me from jumping into the abyss.
It was the second week since the covid symptoms began to appear. The headaches made me feel like my brain was about to explode, and my lungs felt as if they were full cotton obstructing my usually easy breath.

Thinking about by yoga studio being closed since March added more pressure to my head. I tried to teach online in moments of delusion, believing I was feeling better, only to crash on the floor of exhaustion afterward.

Talking took a lot of effort, making it difficult to have any kind of conversations with my fiancé, Fred. Walking to the kitchen to make tea left me breathless and limp. I had texted other teachers a day or two before asking them to cover my classes when Fred gently intervened, telling that I should just take care of myself and rest. He coordinated the substitutes and made sure my zoom yoga classes ran smoothly without me.

I was feeling so bad that at that point I didn't care if the business went bust. Then, I realized I needed to be honest with myself and face these new alien sensations in my body. My back felt broken. My wrists felt hot and inflamed, not moving like they used to. My knees felt arthritic and were difficult to bend. I was constantly urinating, the trips to the bathroom leaving me breathless.

Lying down made me wonder if I was going to lose my battle against corona. It certainly felt that way. My daughter kept pressing me to go to the hospital.

My blood pressure cuff and thermometer still hadn't been delivered. My oximeter was due to arrive the next week. I hoped I would make it. Going to the hospital was out of the question since I didn't have health insurance. Even if I did, I wouldn't want to. They would probably not give me spring water or let me do yoga or have the teas and herbs my body needed. They would've poison me with their lifeless food in single use containers, and I'd be forced to eat it with plastic utensils covered in plastic film. I can't contribute to the landfills.

But the worst part would be not being able to sleep. Hospital rooms are not dark, the nurses loud, it's always freezing, and who knows who my roommate would've been. Lack of sleep wouldn't have allowed my natural healing processes to work to get this thing out of me. I was going to be a prisoner to their schedules, which wouldn't take into consideration my natural circadian rhythms.

However, I could make it all go away if I just happened to fly off the balcony of my 8th floor apartment. The agony of living would disappear. The uncertainty of not knowing if I would be able to pay my rent, to keep my business tore me apart. If I couldn't, where would I end up? What if this virus entity in me was here to take me away anyway?

In my mind I saw my children's faces and snapped out of it.

I got up and slowly walked to my yoga mat. With my unbendable knees, I got down on all fours, and positioned myself into my faithful downward facing dog pose (Adho Mukha Svanasana in Sanskrit) with a bolster under my head, trying to ease all the pains inside my head. The soft bolster supporting my head immediately washes away the delirium.

I recognized the familiar feeling of hopelessness and surrender. The fear of living in incertitude. The feeling of shattered nerves sent me back in time to my 29-year-old self, when I had deep postpartum depression after my third child was born. I had asked my husband to put a lock on the door and put the key in another room so that our preschool daughters wouldn't go out into our 6th floor balcony. It had been for me.

Back into my stance, I bowed down into dog pose, lifting my hips and placing my heart above my head. Something quiet overtook my mental chatter, until I became shaky and had to come down. The pose helped. My mental activity subsided. I felt a little dizzy, but went up again and again, confused about what was happening to my body. I had never experienced all those new physical sensations. Something was different. I used to be able to "tell my dog" to stay for five minutes. Now I couldn't, but something inside of me expanded, and it was not just my inflamed endothelial cells.

I rested into the comfort of a supported child's pose, and my brain became innocent again. Having the bolster under my chest brought me a comfort that reminded me of my mother's loving hug. I was missing her so much and wished she wasn't in another country. The posture and the memory of my mother supported my tender heart and gave me hope. Even adults, sometimes just want their mommy.

Toxic and disorganized thoughts filled with sadness spilled onto the bolster in the form of tears. The tar-like destructive thoughts that almost consumed me, were replaced by a tiny flame in my heart cave that was desperate to grow. I had wanted to go to the balcony and end it all, but I had no energy to walk to the balcony, let alone open the heavy sliding glass door. As I rest in child's pose, (Adho Mukha Virasana) my mind was led to the soothing hug of the pillow holding up my heart and belly. Then my mind wobbled to remind me of my Catholic upbringing. "If you jump, you will go to hell." Then bounced to the yogic teachings, "If you commit suicide, you will have to deal with the karma, paying for each and every individual that you hurt, and then have to come back in another lifetime anyway."

The thought of having to start my life all over again, and the possibility of having to end up with my ex-husband again with added karmic debts gave me the clarity to know that if that could even be a fraction of a possibility, I'd wait it out. No balcony for me. No forced ending. If I died of this virus naturally, that would have been my destiny. But in the meantime, I would shift my mind every time I needed to re-focus. Recalibrate, so that when the inevitable thoughts of permanently quitting this life emerged, I changed my position. If it worked for yoga master BKS Iyengar, who was suicidal at one point in his life, it could work for me.

My downward dog joins me upon command and scares away the monsters that come out to haunt me, and comes between me and the balcony. Good Puppy.

LOVE AT LAST

TERRY TRACHT

I wanted to tell you the truth
and it was tough to do,
as you were not my only man.

No matter how hard I'd try,
it came out as a lie.
There were others before,
men I happened to adore.

Love used to be a game.
Now things just aren't the same.
When I met you, my hunting days were through.

You are my kind of man.
You accept me for who I am.
And for me that is something new.

True happiness I have found.
There's no need to fool around.
You are kind, warm and caring.

I must leave my past behind.
No more mountains left to climb.
With you the future I plan on sharing.

No one knows what life has in store.
But now, for love, I search no more.

NEVER TOO OLD TO YEARN

EVA MARIA KALMAN

The big yellow school bus pulled into the parking lot to let us off at the end of a high school class trip. It was a stifling day at the end of May, and we had been up since the crack of dawn. We were all tired, bored, and grumpy. After hours on the bouncing bus and countless rounds of "99 Bottles of Beer on the Wall," we were glad to see our mothers waiting to take us home.

As the bus lurched to a stop, I looked at the waiting women. They were gathered in small groups, chatting, and smiling. I tried to guess which mother would claim which child. My mother was standing some distance apart, alone. I looked at her and thought she was old. She was fifty with a thickening body, frizzy hair dyed red, no makeup, and a shapeless gray housedress with a row of huge yellow sunflowers marching down the front. I was sixteen and wanted to fit in with the popular girls. I was embarrassed about how my mother looked.

I swore I would never look like that. I promised myself a life filled with good times and joy. And most of all, love. I was going to find my soulmate and live happily ever after.

It didn't work out that way. Despite much hard work, I hadn't reached any of my goals. Many false starts, disappointments, and two failed marriages later, I was in therapy and taking antidepressants.

Recently, I complained to a good friend about my empty life. She reminded me of an old Italian proverb, "One is never too old to yearn." Hearing those simple words stopped me in my tracks and made me think. I recalled when I thought my mother was so old at fifty, back on that sweltering day in May 1961.

I am now twenty-five years older than my mother was at the time. She had a hard life. Her entire family was killed by the Nazis in Hungary. She lost her husband to cancer and was left with two young girls to raise under a Communist regime. Emigrating to the United States and living here was much more difficult than she could ever have imagined. No wonder she looked old.

Had she given up, or did she yearn for more?

As I approach my 76th birthday, I think about aging and what it means. The changes it brings-- limitations, maturity, understanding, and acceptance. The past cannot be changed, and the future is a mystery.

The one thing I do know is that I am still yearning. For love. For closeness. Even for passion. I still want to find my soulmate, a man who makes me happy.

In my mind's eye, we have fascinating conversations and share our thoughts and emotions. We accept --sometimes revel-- in our differences and imperfections. Discoveries delight us. We hold hands and laugh. Then there is the passion. Cuddling and soft kisses are wonderful, and what comes after even better. The inroads time has made on our bodies are forgiven. We're amazed that it's possible to feel like this at our age. We smile and tell each other, "old people don't do this." But we know better. They do. And we do because we have not stopped yearning.

THE COLD OF THE WARMTH
A CHILDHOOD FAMILY TRADITION

IRENE SPERBER

*M*om had a serious Christmas thing. It had to be perfect. No one else cared a figgy, but every year, there she was, creating the precise holiday which forever failed to behave.

One year, a photographer was called in to document our love and warm perfection. Mom rustled around in her long-sleeved, cocktail-length, ex-actress black taffeta dress, the one with the full skirt sporting a deep slit revealing a vicious red on red taffeta petticoat. It made a statement.

My five-year-old self decided to acquire one of my signature colds which caused the right eye to run excessively, turn red and swell up. It must've had a direct link to the right sinus and rendered me unable to look at the dimmest of lights without severe discomfort followed quickly by more waterworks.

So there I was, front and center clutching a teddy bear while facing backward to the camera and bright, bright lights. My white hair bow had slipped down, giving the distinct impression, from that angle, that I was blindfolded, as Mom smiled broadly forward with her best actress face.

My father could not be bothered to shop or think about his role in the holiday cheer. Mom would carefully shop for a peignoir set or other girly attire, wrap it beautifully and attach a loving note from "Dad".

Opening the gift on Christmas morning came with a translucent faux genuine glow. My brother and I ripped open our Santa gifts one by one while this telanovela was playing out behind us. Wait. We did not rip open anything. We had to...and I know I'm overusing this word...*carefully* peel off the tape and open the gift without spoiling the wrapping paper. The paper was...again....*carefully* folded for re-using at next years farce fest.

After opening her gift with her best-est surprised-and-thrilled face (all one word), she lunged across the room to give Dad a big kiss and thank you. At least he had the wherewithal to look sheepish. How that did not cure him of his holiday oversight is beyond me. Even at a very young age, I pretty much sensed this was curious behavior at best.

As this scene played out year after year, my perception of the female role slowly altered right there under the Christmas tree.

Living under the shroud of a make-believe fair and just marriage could most definitely been the ingredients to my jaded adult attitude regarding romance right out of the gate. I experienced the difficulties that made up everyday life in our house, culminating in an occasional nauseating gooey oversized lacy heart card that arrived unsolicited on Valentine's Day.

Unreal role play made it difficult to accept maternal suggestions as to how to act. I recall my exact snarky teen thought: "...and this corrected behavior would get me where exactly?"

I made a conscious note around tween age to ever, never, take the accepted/expected female role on this earth.

THE SEXUAL JOURNEY OF A FIFTIES GIRL

PATRICE DEMERS KANEDA

1982

The phone rang in our condo in Ashiya, Japan. I answered. It was him.

"I'll be home around seven tonight. Getting home early for a change."

I was pleased. "Tell you what. Don't come home," I said in my sexiest voice. "I'll walk down to Route Two to Tony Roma's, but I'll stand outside right near the parking lot, and you can meet me there for dinner. I will just be wearing my London Fog raincoat with nothing underneath. Just pretend that I'm a hooker. How does that sound?"

"Great! See you there." He was always ready for the games.

How did I become this person? Me, a fifties girl born in 1935. Me, the parochial schoolgirl who'd had a shrine in her bedroom. Me, the girl who'd run away from boys who were interested in her? Poor Andy, who'd taken me to the ball at Girls State. When I saw him coming toward me on the sidewalk the next day, I ran in the opposite direction.

He was a better runner, and he caught up with me. "What's wrong?"

"Oh, nothing. I didn't see you. Just getting some exercise."

And then there was David, who'd taken me to the prom. I didn't like the feel of his hand on my waist. When we reached my house after the dance, I said a quick goodbye, ran into the house, and locked the door. My mother quickly unlocked it and let him in, along with the other couple. She had planned an after-party since it was my birthday.

In my senior year, I was allowed to leave school for the afternoon to volunteer at Democratic headquarters. Stevenson was running. There, I met my husband-to-be. He was twenty-six, and I was seventeen. We chatted. I was interested. He went to foreign movies, to the beach at Watch Hill, and to plays. This would do.

When she heard of our engagement, my favorite auntie said, "Oh, Patty. Save yourself for your wedding night. He'll always respect you for it. Your uncle didn't touch me for three nights. I cried so much."

By that time, I was interested in more than that. We were doing a lot of heavy petting and had some pretty intimate swims in a moonlit lake, but I was still a virgin. We were married when I was twenty and a junior in college. There were many happy years, years when the marriage was like air. We restored an eighteenth-century house. We had children. We just were, like the characters in the book *The Unbearable Lightness of Being*, but storm clouds were gathering.

I guess it was the feminist movement and that summer at Ferry Beach in Saco, Maine, at the Unitarian campground that opened my eyes. The year was 1972. I was there with my thirteen-year-old daughter and my four-year-old son. My husband drove up from Connecticut on weekends.

While our children were involved in activities, we women held feminist circles. Our leader was single, pretty, blond, overweight, middle-aged, and proud of her body. She walked around the camp in her bikini or shorts and a halter top as if flaunting her midriff bulge like a wealthy Bengali woman, except that her breasts were spilling over her top. She spoke freely about her many lovers.

When we gathered, we sat in a circle and waited for the word that would be our topic. Each of us in turn, spoke to it, saying whatever entered our minds. No one could interrupt. Topics could be money, food, jobs, sex, children, friends, household chores... whatever. We spoke freely. For many of us, it was the first time we'd even thought about those topics.

Most of us were virgins—or sort of virgins—when we married. We had done a lot of fooling around in the back seats of cars, necking, petting, things with our hands, and things with our mouths. Things we didn't have words for. There was no penetration. That was much too dangerous.

Birth control was illegal, and in Catholic Boston, a proponent of birth control had been arrested just for showing condoms. It was the time of illegal abortions and many deaths as a result. The stigma of getting pregnant before marriage was horrendous. Some girls committed suicide or, more commonly, went away for a while and gave their babies up for adoption. Others just bore the shame of whispers and comments about the child born out of wedlock or the girl who'd had a shotgun wedding.

One woman in our group, an Italian American, didn't even know about intercourse until her honeymoon. She'd gotten a big surprise on her wedding night. Later in the summer, it was nice to see her walking off to the beach with her husband in the evening with a mat and a smile on her face.

As the Virginia Slims ad said, "You've come a long way, baby."

We read Betty Friedan, *The Joy of Sex*, Simone de Beauvoir, and Anais Nin. We saw films like *An Unmarried Woman* and the TV series *Diary of a Marriage* with Luv Ullman.

I took a feminist course at the University of Connecticut. Gloria Steinem was one of our speakers. We were encouraged to buy peacock feathers and vibrators and to learn how to use them to please our partners and ourselves. Unfortunately, I missed one class where we were going to examine our vaginas with a speculum. I was busy that day but told the group I was skipping because I didn't want to be the oldest vagina there. That word, *vagina*, was just one of the words we used to describe our sexual organs. *Clitoris* and *ovaries* were new to us. Later, the show *Vagina Monologues* would deal with those terms.

Our husbands hated to hear about those meetings. It was all very threatening to them. They were being asked to do half of the household chores and to do things like taking their children to the dentist or after-school sports. We were teachers, nurses, secretaries, and professors, and we'd been carrying the entire burden of childcare and the home. Now, we were even asking our mates to please us during sex rather than just pleasing themselves. This was a revolution.

I got a divorce and moved to a small planned community, originally with my Japanese lover, but he went back to Japan. Within a year, everyone on my street was divorced. It was like wildfire. Women were knocking on my door for advice and lining up outside my classroom to talk to me about their marital problems. Time passed. I learned to live alone. I embraced my sexuality. My lover came back and became my husband. That's how I got to Tony Roma's, wearing a London Fog raincoat.

We walked into the restaurant, and the waiter asked if he could take my coat. I answered, "No thank you" and smiled at my husband.

HARRY

MARILYN LIEBERMAN

The elevator gave an unfamiliar lurch, enough for Harry to feel a wayward heartbeat before it glided to an effortless stop. Slowly, Harry entered the lobby of his 30-story apartment building. The cavernous space no longer shared the sounds of shuffling feet hurrying toward the door.

As he did every morning, Harry dressed in a suit. Although retired for several years, he resisted the more comfortable sweat suit. It reminded him of pajamas and punctured the American image he craved. His silk tie glistened as he walked underneath the ornate chandelier.

"Hi John," he greeted the uniformed doorman with an easy familiarity.

"Hi Harry, nice morning," the doorman responded.

A whiff of spring air caught him by surprise. He noticed the dainty pink and white flower heads that dotted the perimeter of the building. Same as last year he thought. It was not a welcome memory. He did not want to be reminded. It was last year that his wife of forever had passed on.

"Do you need help buddy?" a worker filling potholes asked as

Harry shuffled onto the sidewalk under the building's imposing portico.

"No thank you," Harry replied waving his cane in the air.

A story he never tired of telling, Harry knew from the moment he saw her on the ship of fractured souls that he would marry her. Brash, racing toward life, defying memories from the past, Malke was worn and suspicious; they found if not passion, an easy intimacy with each other. It proved to be more than enough.

And so by saying yes to each other and burying the ashes of the past, they, with more than a little cunning and charm, managed to build a successful business together.

Two sons were soon celebrated by a community of friends.

And without warning, life is just that way, the youngest son at age 24 passed away from an undiagnosed rare cancer. His sneakers still lay in the corner of the closet when the older brother was the victim of a tragic ski accident.

Harry and Malke were now spectators, sidelined as they answered invitations that came with amazing regularity, births, graduations, engagements, weddings.

It was at night when the blinds were closed and Harry could no longer see the lights of the Greek café across the street that he would stroke his wife's soft thighs and allow his tears to flow.

And in the morning Malke would shout, "Do you have the bar mitzvah gift for the Adlers?" Harry would smile and waive the check in the air.

"Harry, I need to go to the beauty parlor."

"OK Malke, I'll call for the car."

"Call now," she demanded, as she struggled to close the zipper on her dress.

These thoughts filled his mind as he neared the park. Not really a park, some benches, a few bare trees, clumps of grass weakened by the winter's snowstorms.

He sat down on a bench and watched a young Korean child dressed in wide trousers run to catch a large puffy ball. His parents, lean and young, clapped in delight. "Catch it, catch it," they cried.

Harry looked at the young couple and wondered how such an ordinary event could be taken for granted. How strange, that in this bleak moment, as he watched the young father embrace his son, that Harry should feel closer to humanity than he had felt in a long time.

HANDSTANDS

ROSA SANTANA

"Everybody, go up now," I instructed as I came down from a handstand on the pink wall of the studio I'd opened. It was a full mixed-level class on a sunny Saturday morning.

"I can't do that. My brittle bones will break!" Rhoda said, with her hunched back and rounded shoulders.

Esther complained, "I'm scared for my arthritic shoulders."

"I don't want to do a handstand," Madeline added in her Brooklyn accent.

Extending my arm forcefully to direct the students away from the wall, I snapped, "All of you that are not interested in progressing in your yoga practice, go to the short wall and do a downward-facing dog pose. I can help you improve and grow, but if you don't want to, I don't know why you're here!"

One third of the class walked slowly to the short wall. I continued teaching the handstanders. Once I got them up a few times and responded to the various levels of handstanders, I looked at the group doing dog pose. I really didn't give them too much attention because they had annoyed me. I knew some of them could do handstands, and I could help them, if they would only let go of fear.

After class, Madeline, whom I had gotten to know outside of class, asked if she could have a word with me, in private. When the studio cleared out, she stood in front of me with her feet wide apart and her hands on her hips. Her usual smile vanished, but her gaze pierced mine. She took a deep breath and adjusted her blond hair behind her ear.

"What the hell is wrong with you? Forcing us old ladies to do handstands! We know you want to evolve. We see your growth. We want to continue witnessing your progress. But none of us want to be teachers," she said, gesturing with her hands, something she often did. "We come to yoga to feel better. To see our friends. To become better people. You can't treat us like that. Do you want to lose all of us old ladies? We love your classes, but recently, you've become a real pain in the ass. We don't have to do handstands. Ever. For no reason. And you have no right to try and force us."

My stomach turned. My heart started to race, and I felt frozen. I had not realized my behavior. What the hell had become of me? Putting aside the yoga teacher role, who was I becoming as a person?

Then I had a flashback of myself at home with Matteo's spit sprinkling onto my face as he bellowed insults at me while I stood paralyzed. I realized at that moment what was happening. I was being bullied at home, where I had no voice. At home, I felt stupid and incompetent. At the studio, I was in charge. My repressed anger was spilling over onto my students. My pain was leading my classes. My unworthiness was lashing out in the sacred yoga space I had built.

After Madeline left, I sat cross-legged in the middle of the wood floor, feeling heavy and alone. The energy of the pain I had caused was floating in the air, and I realized it belonged to me. It was cold. I was cold. My head hung low, and my chest caved in to protect the void in my heart. My throat had become a dam that couldn't open at home. Years of holding in tears, sadness, and disappointment began to erupt from my empty heart.

The dam opened, and years of hoarded tears, full of poison, toxins, and insults, flowed into my eyes and down my cheeks. My body shook as oceans of tears and loud cries inundated my various emotions. I was a failure in my marriage and in my career, and even the stiffness and scoliosis in my body kept me from moving along in some yoga poses.

My outward strength was a sham. My leadership skills were just hiding the insecurity I have lived with all my life. After surrendering to the tears and allowing my body and mind to come together and express themselves without judgement, the hurricane of emotions subsided. Those tears were like vomit that needed to come out. The much-needed tears pulled out emotional tartar from my being.

Madeline had made me realize I wasn't following the yogic teachings of non-violence that were directing my path. I was embarrassed. I was ashamed. I questioned some of the techniques in my training in which there was an emphasis on making sure the teacher had command of the class, to make sure the students would do what the teacher said. If I didn't follow that paradigm, I could fail the next certification test. Perhaps, I hadn't found that fine line between maintaining control and being a jerk. I was a jerk. As I learned to take command of my classes, I'd become a bully. They say bullied people become bullies.

I was in the process of deciding to end my marriage of twenty years, and the toxicity of my indecision had polluted my teaching. As difficult as it was to realize how I was not serving my students properly, I was grateful for Madeline's commitment to our friendship by pointing out to me what I could not see. I called those students and apologized. I didn't want them to have a bad taste of yoga because of me. I couldn't bear the idea of them giving up yoga because of my arrogance and ignorance.

Luckily, they came back the following week, and since then, I've given up the idea that everyone has to do handstands. I give them options, and I realize the pose being done is not that important. One group can do handstands, and the other group dog pose, and everyone benefits. Not everyone wants to be a yoga teacher, and not everyone should be doing handstands. I know that. I know alternatives, I know modifications, and now, I have put aside my ego and gained more experience in class control. I have nothing to prove.

Since then, I've passed many levels of certification tests. The years of taking abuse are over. I divorced Matteo, and I am still healing from the emotional blows. I don't take out my frustrations on students anymore, thanks to my very dear friend, Madeline. She still tells me the truth, and I love her for it.

The purpose of yoga is to quiet the mind so we can have a vision of the soul. Handstands or any other yoga poses can be a tool for transformation to train the mind into a state of silence. I still teach my students to go up, but not necessarily into handstands. Now, I elevate my students with encouraging and inspiring words.

"Those of you that can do a handstand, go up. The rest of you, come to this wall with me, and you will do the same arm actions of handstand in the following modifications."

Now, all my students can deepen their understanding of yoga in their own way. I give options, and the room is more peaceful for all of us.

MOVING ON

TERRY TRACHT

It's finally happened and you did it all alone.
The time had come for you to leave home.
It was years in the making and very painstaking,
But now there was no doubt-
you were going to move out.

You searched high and low for a place you'd like to go.
Not just anywhere would do.
North Miami, Miami Shores and Wynwood were too
far from the action for you.

You finally found a condo on South Beach,
where all of the clubs and young people were within your reach.
Your father and I met the news with glee.
We delighted in the thought that we'd finally be free.

After one year of living there alone,
you fell in love and moved into your girlfriend's home.

It wasn't hard for anyone to see that you and she were meant to be.
You, the little boy that I used to carry,
were all grown up and going to get married.
You exchanged vows with your beautiful wife,
and then moved on to start a new life.
It hasn't been that long since you've been gone,
yet I feel so alone with just the two of us at home.

I miss you asking me about my day.
I miss seeing your car in the driveway.
I'll miss you taking the puppy for her morning walks.
I'll miss going to movie premieres with you and our late-night talks.

There are no more shoes by the door.
No full laundry baskets on the floor.
I take a look at your empty chair.
I envision your smile, and you aren't there.

MY LIFT

DR. JOYCE ZARITSKY

Standing in front of my building, I am waiting impatiently for my lift at seven o'clock in the evening. Finally, it pulls up. I check its credentials on my phone. The driver is supposed to be Danny, the license plate matches, and it's a red Toyota. Everything is a "go." I know for sure it's for me. I am going to a party where I will see some friends I haven't seen in a while and am anticipating a lovely evening. It is raining and getting dark. I am annoyed I didn't bring an umbrella, but hopefully, the driver will drop me in front of the building so I won't get very wet.

I run over to the car and start to get in. A voice says, "Hello, Susan. Welcome. I'm Danny. Glad to be your driver." As I take my seat, the car starts moving I look over at the driver's seat to glance at my driver. But no one is there. Is it just the darkness or is the driver's seat really empty?

"Where are you?" I ask. "Where is my driver?"

"Not to worry. I am Danny. Your driver. You are in an automatic vehicle. I am a robot, a remote driver… a computer who will be taking you where you are going." He recites the address.

"I want to get out," I say. "I want a real live driver, not a robot. "

"Don't worry. The research is clear. We robot drivers are safer than humans. Many fewer mishaps, what you humans call accidents."

"I don't care about your research. I want a live driver. Why didn't anyone tell me about this arrangement?"

"My company was supposed to notify you. Didn't they?"

"No, not at all." I glance out the window. The car is moving at a fairly fast clip. I grasp and clutch the end of the seat belt.

"I want to get out!" I yell, feeling my blood pressure rising rapidly. "This is crazy."

"Can't let you out here, too dangerous." Danny says.

"I don't want to die in your car. Let me out."

"Sit back and relax. We are almost there." He repeats the address I'm going to.

I take a deep breath. I am going to die. I know it.

We stop at a light. I try to open the door, but it is locked. I look at surrounding vehicles and see drivers staring at my car. They know. They can see that there is no one in the driver's seat. Should I yell or pound on the window? But I don't. I am resigned to my fate. I am going to die. There is no turning around.

When the car pulls up to my destination, I touch my body to check that I am still alive. Everything in my body seems to be in its right place, except I can hear my heart pounding.

"Before you get out," Danny says.

I take a deep breath and whisper in a voice that sounds strangely hoarse. "What?"

"My company has a new service."

"What is it?" Now that we are parked, my voice sounds more normal.

"We can provide car happiness. All remotely of course."

"What are you talking about?"

"I have a way of arousing you and can give you a 'happy ending.' Everyone who has tried it so far says it's wonderful. And as a promotion, we are offering it without charge. You won't pay a penny more than your regular fare."

"That's crazy."

"Maybe, but these days, people are lonely, stuck in their homes.

Alone. So sad. And my company has started offering this extra service. Don't you want to try it?"

"How does it work?" I ask, my curiosity piqued.

"Lady, I can't take the time to go into how I work or how our computers work. I'll be dammed if I can explain it anyway. I'm just a computer, you know. Not a computer scientist. But if you try it and fill out our online questionnaire afterward, we have a special offer. Want to hear about it?"

He doesn't wait for me to answer and continues, "And to boot, it doesn't take that much time. You will enjoy yourself and still be on time."

I glance at my watch. It is only seven thirty. I am at least a half hour early. What is there to lose?

"Okay," I murmur, wondering with great curiosity what I am getting myself into.

Suddenly, the car windows darken. I am shrouded in darkness, and a song with a man's voice starts to play. The car starts rocking, and I feel my body vibrating to the music. I can just make out the words. In addition, there is a perfumed odor filling the air. A soft curtain drops down in front of me so that no one can see in.

"Let me in, darling," the voice in the song sings. "I know you are waiting for me to enter. We can have a good time and come together. You are my center. Are you ready to be pleasured? What is there to lose? Let me in. Let me in. I want to pleasure you, and I know you will be pleasured also. Just relax and enjoy."

Suddenly, something hard rises from the seat I am in. I can feel my legs opening and realize I am becoming aroused. More and more. More and more. Inside the curtain, I feel hands touching and massaging my breasts.

"Are you loving it? Are you wet yet?" the voice sings. "I know you are. Let's make it last, last. You are my lovey. This is fantastic."

To my surprise, my body starts to rise to meet this hard object, and I can feel myself ready to come. My eyes are closed. I'm not even sure where I am.

"Are you ready? Are you ready?" the voice sings. "Of course, you are. I know it. Are you ready for a happy ending? I know the answer."

"I'm ready, ready, ready," I whisper.

After I don't know how long, the lights in the car come on, the curtain disappears, the music stops, and the rocking stops.

After a short silence, there is a voice that I recognize. It is Danny. "How was that? Did you enjoy yourself? I can tell you did. Everyone we've tried it on has agreed it was great. Much more than a lousy taxi ride."

He unlocks the back door, and before I know it, I am out on the sidewalk in the rain.

I hear Danny's voice: "Goodbye, lovey. Hope you remember to give me a good tip. And don't forget to fill out the questionnaire." The car pulls away from the curb. I feel my body relaxing. And I am wondering, *How did this happen? Did it?* I know the answer.

I pull down my skirt, straighten it, fix my hair, and walk up to the building. I ring the bell then check my watch. It's almost eight thirty.

Will I tell anyone? Should I? Anyway, who would believe me?

SUNRISE

TERRY TRACHT

My husband Roman was born and raised in Tashkent, the capitol of Uzbekistan, a Central Asian nation and former Soviet republic. Uzbekistan borders on Turkmenistan, Tajikistan and Afganistan, and is one of only two countries in the world which is doubly landlocked. Eighty percent of the country's territory is comprised of monotonous desert, and the only visible bodies of water there are occasional lakes and man-made reservoirs. Roman only knew what the Baltic Sea and the Atlantic and Pacific Oceans looked like from maps. He could never imagine experiencing the sea firsthand.

Because Roman considered cruise ships to be "floating prisons with lots of food," it took me months of coaxing to convince him to book us on a seven-day voyage to the Caribbean. We sailed aboard Royal Caribbean's *Oasis of the Seas*, which accommodates 5,600 travelers and is one of the largest passenger ships in the world.

Roman was left wide-eyed by the vessel's five saltwater pools, gigantic twisting water slide, three whirlpools and its "Central Park" themed boardwalk, but being a Uzbek stoic, he did not express his approval. We had a balcony cabin on the seventh deck. It was tighter than we expected, but comfortable enough for two, and it was appointed with amenities such as down pillows, plush terry cloth bathrobes, soft slippers and Penhaligon soaps.

During our first dinner aboard, we savored a scrumptious buffet of culinary delights ranging from shrimp tacos to Peking duck to delicious, rare roast beef. This was accompanied by a vast selection of fresh salads, tropical fruits, free flowing soft ice cream and mouthwatering desserts such as seven-layer caramel cake and white chocolate mousse. Roman didn't admit it, but by his several trips to the dessert station, I knew he was impressed. After dinner, we headed to the Opal Theater, where we enjoyed a lavish stage production of the Broadway musical "CATS" from our plush, red velvet seats. To top the evening off, we relaxed over frozen piña coladas in the 24-hour cocktail lounge adjacent to the Casino. By 1:30 a.m., we were bushed and called it a night.

On our first morning at sea, I awakened to a sliver of bright light seeping between our slightly drawn curtains. I pulled open the long silk drapes and was captivated by an intoxicating sight I had rarely experienced from such a vantage point.

My eyes scanned an expansive, powder-blue sky dotted with puffs of billowing cotton. After a few moments, I watched in awe as a golden glow crept over the horizon. Then, ever so slowly, it emerged- a fiery coral orb. Its rays radiated from its core, illuminating the sea below.

I had to adjust to the brightness of the orange sphere from the comparative darkness of our cabin. My eyes ached as I stared at it, but I could not look away. I was mesmerized by the vision and felt it would be selfish of me not to share the moment with my husband. I approached my sleeping partner, leaned in, and called his name. I had learned a long time ago, the hard way, not to touch him while he slept.

"Honey, wake up and come to the balcony. You have got to see this sunrise," I said.

He was lying face down on his stomach, his long dark-brown hair teasing his bare, broad shoulders. He didn't respond. After a few moments, I gingerly called his name again. He did not move, but with a voice muffled by his pillow, he muttered, "I don't know why you bother me with these things. They have better ones in Tashkent."

THE SILENT WARRIOR

ROSA SANTANA

*H*e hung up the phone on me. I was trying to remind him of our agreement. After 20 years of not being heard and three attempts to separate, I finally decided to divorce him. I got tired of his frequent trips to Brazil, which usually corresponded with his birthday and carnival. I was fed up with his lack of respect towards our three daughters and me. Perhaps all the yoga warrior poses gave me the strength and clarity of mind. "I am worthy of a better life." I always wondered why there were three warrior poses, and I realized we all have battles to face.

He decided to move back in June instead of August like we had agreed, and I had one week to move out. My neck became tense at the idea of facing him again.

My youngest daughter had decided to live with me, and I would lend her my car to drive 30 miles to school every day. She knew that it was easier to coordinate any schedule with me than with her father. He was not always reliable. Like the days he promised to drive her to school only to change his mind last minute and yelling at me to take her. But, I was used to it, so I was always ready.

What I was not ready for was a move. I still hadn't found a place to live. My father kept promising to buy me a house, but none of the houses that I found were good enough based on his standards. I had a hard time concentrating. There were so many details to take care of. Gather my belongings. Pack. Separate my name from all the joint accounts. Follow up on the court papers. Remember to eat. Find a house. Find another one. My mom keeps asking me if I found a place.

At 47 years old, I shouldn't need my daddy to buy me a house. I should have much more in my bank accounts had my ex-husband not cleaned them all out before he fled the country. By now, my business should be turning a much better profit than it has. And my youngest needs more money for college applications. Do I have enough money to rent an apartment? My mind cannot look at any more houses. I already found five that were perfect. It's not so easy buying a home when you have no money and can't focus.

"Mom, Dad, please fly here and look at houses, and buy the one you like. It will be easier if you are here. We have to think about who will take care of you once you can't take care of yourselves. We can find a property where there is space for both of you, and by then your three granddaughters will be old enough to help take care of you." My mind switches back to the girls. "They need money for college, and soon my youngest will too. I need to keep it together for their sake. I have a headache. Oh, I guess I forgot to eat."

June 1st finally arrived. My nightmare of an ex-husband landed. It should take him at least an hour to get to the house. That's how much time I had to leave. Except I had nowhere to go. Most of my important belongings are my children's baby books and yoga books. At least they're safe in storage. I started slowly when he was still here, fearing one of his deranged episodes when he would force us into a room and throw away our things. My daughter is still haunted by memories of watching him from the bedroom window take out her bike to a pile of our things on the curb. Her tears did not move him. "The little girl that picked up the bike is so happy! Look how your bike will bring joy to that little girl. We will get you a new one that's a little bigger," I said in an attempt to console her. She was not convinced, and her bike was never replaced.

The last thing I packed into my white Honda Accord was a

laundry basket with my pillow. I had nowhere to go. My daughter, who was staying at the house, for the time being, asked me if I'd be okay. I held back the tears of being forced out of the home I thought would be my permanent one. I didn't want her to worry. As she helped me bring the last suitcase to my car, she offered to make me breakfast, but my stomach was tied in knots all the way to my throat. "That's okay. I'm meeting a friend for breakfast. "It was a lie. I was all alone and too ashamed to tell anyone.

After 20 years of emotional torture, it was finally over. I drove away with the remnants of my married life stuffed into my car. I was shaky, and my vision became blurred by tears. I felt unsafe driving. I stopped at a nearby diner and sat in a booth all by myself. It was 7am.

The waitress didn't even ask. She brought me coffee. As I gazed bleary-eyed out the window, I couldn't imagine where my life would take me. I had mustered the strength to finally say no to the abuse, yet my crushed heart lay on the dirty diner floor.

I held back tears as I ordered the breakfast special. It was only six dollars. I don't know if the coffee was terrible because of my tears or because it was really vile diner coffee. The waitress was so sweet and told me it was a fresh pot. I drank it anyway so that I wouldn't hurt her feelings. The whole meal stayed in my throat for hours.

As I drove around aimlessly, I remembered some students of mine were going back home to Europe for a month. So I called them and asked if they needed someone to water their plants and get the mail while they were gone. Without me having to explain, they understood my situation and invited me over. Thank goodness they left that afternoon. They didn't see me crying for the next 30 days.

Reorganizing their Tupperware and deep cleaning their kitchen kept me sane for the first few days. Some days I didn't teach. I stayed in the apartment on the kitchen floor in a fetal position or crying in the living room. When I practiced yoga, every pose made me cry, or I felt shaky. I couldn't even balance in headstand, which was one of my favorite poses. I questioned my decision. Maybe it wasn't so bad. Perhaps he was right. I am stupid. My mind would go back to scenes from my life with him. I knew that movie very well. Insults, tirades, tears, then flowers, gifts, begging for forgiveness. The intimate partner violence and abuse that never ends, regardless of how many times you pray, visualize and hope it will change.

    Some days I had to put my memories and trauma into words to clear them out of my head. Other days it was dancing or chanting mantras that would help clear out the painful noise in my head. Other days I couldn't pick myself off the floor.

I finally gathered the strength and courage to call my parents and ask for help. I told them I was running out of time and wasn't in the emotional state to buy a house without any money. I asked if they would help me rent an apartment. I was so grateful that they did.

    I found a two-bedroom apartment walking distance from my yoga studio so that my daughter and I could share the Accord. Although I had no credit (thanks to my ex) and didn't make enough for the apartment, my realtor wrote a letter to the owner about my situation. The apartment owner was a good man and took pity on my story. So, with first, last, and two months' worth of a security deposit, my daughter and I moved in on July 1st.

    I sat down on my bed with her in our otherwise empty apartment, and I said to her, "Listen." She looked at me and answered, "I don't hear anything." "That's what peace sounds like, I exhaled. "Welcome to our new life. "

MY MOTHER'S ONE-NIGHT STAND

EVA MARIA KALMAN

I liked living in the refugee camp. For a curious ten-year old, it was an exciting adventure. When my mother, younger sister, Erika, and I arrived from a small village at the Hungarian/Austrian border, we were assigned to a large and sunny room. Two rows of 15 wooden beds lined the unadorned whitewashed walls. Identical gray blankets were stretched over clean white sheets. Despite the regimental surroundings, the room was filled with the lively chatter and laughter of women. They greeted us warmly and since there were no other children, they made a fuss over the two cute little girls who would be staying with them. I looked around and wondered 'Where are the men?' To my relief, there weren't any. This building was reserved for women who had made the long and dangerous journey across the border from Hungary to Austria alone.

After the introductions, we put away our few belongings, found three beds next to each other and got settled. My mother told me we were very lucky to have been put into the "women's quarters."

. . .

Within a few days I gained enough confidence to explore my surroundings. I learned that we, along with hundreds of other refugees who had escaped the ill-fated Hungarian Revolution of 1956, were sheltered on an old army base just outside of Vienna, Austria. Always curious, I peeked into the other barracks in the camp. The one-story red brick buildings were identical, but the interiors weren't at all like the one I was in. They were dark, noisy and strange smelling. These were what we called "the family quarters," occupied by as many as eight to ten families- mother, father and children. Blankets strung on clothes lines divided the large open spaces into little cubicles. While the blankets provided visual privacy, nothing could block the sounds and smells of too many people crammed into too small a space.

When I got tired of snooping around, I was happy to be back in the "women's quarters" where it was clean and quiet. My mother was right- we were lucky indeed! The women got along well (most of the time, anyway) and my sister and I had a lot of "aunties" to look after us. Like the night Mother didn't come home. My sister was only five, and didn't notice that Mom wasn't there at bedtime. The grownups didn't seem concerned, so I didn't worry either.

Mom returned the next day, looking happy and excited. This is her story: she was on her way to the American Embassy in Vienna to ask if our visas to the United States had been granted. As she was waiting for the bus, she met a very nice gentleman. He worked at the Embassy and said he was in a position to expedite our visa process. Unfortunately, it was getting late in the day and the Embassy would close shortly. He promised to take her there first thing in the morning. To be there early enough, he put Mom up in a fancy hotel close to the Embassy. The gentleman (who forever remained nameless) sent a fabulous breakfast to her room and waited for her in the lobby. When she stepped out of the elevator, he assured her the room had been paid for and she had nothing to worry about. Soon they arrived at the Embassy, where she was assured that our visas were being expedited.

I don't remember how the women in our bunk reacted to the story, but I do think I was the only one who believed it.

AN ODD JOB ODYSSEY

MANDY URENA

*A*s I reflect on the uncharted, higgledy-piggledy trajectory that has been my career path, I reminisce with humor at my odd odyssey. In the building of my resume, I have unconsciously morphed in and out of various versions of my professional self, switching out my proverbial hats to suit the job and the culture as I worked my way around the world.

At age sixteen, I changed out of my school uniform and into my very first set of work clothes at the prestigious Royal Allesley Hotel in Coventry in England. This hotel was my hometown's version of high-end on the grounds that it hosted the only silver-service carvery in the city. My waitress uniform was a frumpy A-line polyester black skirt paired with a shapeless starched white blouse—an outfit I would not have been seen dead wearing outside of the workplace.

My workload included attending the head chef as he wheeled his carvery trolley of roast turkey, roast pork and roast beef in and out of white linen-draped tables. His job was to slice and plate the meats and my job was to pile on the roast potatoes, Yorkshire puddings and traditionally overcooked English vegetables—all with a silver spoon and a silver fork, using only one hand. Then, I was to ask if Sir and Madam would care for seasoning and gravy.

Seasoning, as every Brit knows, is simply the upscale vernacular for sage and onion stuffing out of a box, but to glam up the dining experience, instead of asking if Madam wanted stuffing, we were trained to say, "would Madam care for any seasoning?" Consequently, every week without exception, some jokester husband would pipe up with "ooh yes, Madge is partial to a good stuffing, aren't you Love?"

The highlight of this, my weekend gig, was a shift meal and leftover cream cakes from the desert trolley; it certainly was not the pitiful wage of $15, cash in hand, for two days of skivvying. After 6 months, it was time to ditch the silver service for the bustling Holyhead Pub around the corner.

Because I was only seventeen, a year shy of the legal drinking age, I could not serve alcohol. Instead, I was to collect glasses. My duties were to squeeze through the crowds of revelers and stack towers of empty pint glasses high in my arms. Clad in jeans and a tight-fitting t-shirt sporting the pub's logo, I was knee-deep in a party atmosphere. I washed my beer glasses until 10.50 pm every evening when the landlady, legally obliged to empty her establishment by 11, would yell, "c'mon lads, drink up. Do your talkin' as you do your walkin'!"

Glass collecting was a paycheck to pass the time and, although educated, what I really yearned for was to be a world traveler with a rucksack on my back. I was not ready to commit to a serious job reserved for responsible adults, and the thought of climbing the rungs of a corporate ladder was as exciting as fishing out a TV dinner from the depths of the freezer.

Oddly, the catalyst that transported me into a globe-trotting life was a random chick flick—a B-movie entitled *Not Quite Jerusalem* in the romance section of the corner video store. It was about a girl who went to Israel as a volunteer in a farming community called a *kibbutz*. Inspired, I did some research and applied to be a volunteer myself. Three months later I had a new job in Haifa, Israel, albeit unpaid.

There, I had an interesting selection of jobs: I could be a cotton picker in the fields; an orange picker in the orchard; a production line worker in the paint factory, or a chicken plucker in the kitchens. What choices! I opted for the paint factory. Even though the work hours were ungodly, and I started at 4 am due to the intense daytime heat, I had my afternoons free to swim at the pool and sunbathe. The only other downside was the uniform—oversized navy-blue hospital-like scrubs. I felt like a shapeless sack of potatoes, a factory reject on the shop floor.

I sat on the assembly line with other volunteers from various parts of the world. We put lids and labels on little pots of primary-colored paint as they traveled along the conveyor belt. After three or four hours of this, to relieve the monotony, we would change to another department and pack children's pastel chalk into cartons for export. If we were lucky, we would help load boxes onto forklift trucks outside.

After three months of factory work, I quit. It was not only the laborious repetitive tasks; it was the eeriness of walking down a mud track between the cotton fields at zero-dark-thirty under the light of the moon. But, if truth be told, seeing a snake for the first time in my life—a half runover Viper still wriggling—was the impetus for me to move on.

A rickety bus transported me four hundred kilometers from the simplicity of my kibbutz life to a glamorous five-star existence at the King Solomon Hotel, situated in the desert oasis that is Eilat on the Red Sea. Eilat was a known work haven for world travelers in the eighties, and I quickly landed a position as a cocktail waitress in a piano bar.

My posh new job meant a classy stylish uniform and on the first day, I swanned into work feeling very aristocratic, finely clad in a real silk, white designer blouse with padded shoulders, and a black drop-waist silk skirt that flowed to the floor, caressing my ankles. I served kosher cocktails with names like Queen Kiss as the Argentinian piano player, who fancied himself as Julio Iglesias, crooned *Begin the Beguine*. I had inadvertently transitioned from broke farm help to well-paid, highly tipped purveyor of exotic drinks.

Eight months into my job, I served a Queen Kiss to a tall,

tanned Californian soldier with a thin moustache and pumped muscular chest. Drawn in by his American charm and his tales of Hollywood, Malibu and the beach life, I decided to follow him to the City of Angels. I immediately found a job at a jazz bar on the beach and inadvertently added to my growing resume.

It was at the Lighthouse Café in Hermosa Beach that I traded serving high-end cocktails for shots of Cuervo Gold and bottles of Corona with lime stuffed in the top. As live bands rocked on stage, I zipped between Pepto-Bismol pink pub tables uniformed in a pink golf shirt, gray short shorts and white sneakers. My job lasted a year, which was a lot longer than my relationship with the soldier, so after a year of loud music ringing in my ears, I decided to move east—to the Far East—to visit my Japanese friend from high school.

There, my work path took a hairpin curve: the jazz bar with pink tables became a corporate board room and I transitioned into a conservative English teacher, well-presented in a classic business suit. In the late eighties, there was an abundance of work for foreigners, so on days when I was not carrying a briefcase full of textbooks and lecturing on the importance of a past participle, I was in the movies or in a TV commercial. In a studio in the center of Tokyo, I morphed into a movie extra on set playing a partygoer in a club scene, or a lawyer in an office scene, and even a hooker on a street corner! I was working twenty-four-seven.

To balance out my obscene work schedule, I decided I needed to find a hobby—something cultural, something typically Japanese—so I enrolled in shiatsu massage school. Little did I know it at the time, but this training would be the concrete that set the foundation for my career. I found joy and passion in my classes, and from here, massage became my life's purpose.

Since Japan, I have been a massage therapist for the last three decades. My workplace has transitioned from the spa to the hospital ward to the chiropractor's office to the casino. But these days, I work in an exclusive country club-esque hotel in the heart of Miami Beach. It's cool; we wear trendy jeans and a plain white t-shirt like James Dean in *Rebel Without a Cause*.

As I cycle to work along the beach in the sunshine, I turn the pages in my head and think about all the other commutes to work over the years. What an odd odyssey my work trajectory has been—as unconventional as any career path could be.

Work makes me happy; I do what I love. Massaging and healing people defines me, and it gives me purpose. But the best part is that, on any given day, it is highly probable that my client will be the most famous football player in the world, a celebrity chef or even British royalty. I have come a long way from, "Would Madam like stuffing?"

ABOUT THE AUTHORS

Funny, sad, rewarding and different - a weekly gathering of eclectically exciting writers who derive tales and poetry from real life and their imagination. This is the Women Writers of South Beach (by alphabetical order).

BARBARA BERG

Though Barbara made her living as a copywriter, she consider herself a jack-of-all-trades, master of none. Her avocations include acting, painting, needlepoint and baking. Her father always said that when it came to writing, she had a "light touch." Barbara hopes this assessment is evident in the stories and musings she posted on her blog, as well as in her books for children and adults.

EVA MARIA KALMAN

Born on the wrong side of the Iron Curtain in Hungary, Eva spent two years in a refugee camp in Austria before coming to the US at the age of 12. A self-professed problem child, she had an inquisitive nature and a creative imagination from an early age. This led to her writing stories—happy and optimistic tales of love, family and intrigue. Her favorite pastimes are people watching, theater and world travel. She lives in Miami with her polydactyl cat, Lulu .

PATRICE DEMERS KANEDA

Patrice Demers Kaneda grew up in the town of Southbridge, Massachusetts which at the time of her childhood was sixty percent Quebecois. She moved to Connecticut at the age of thirteen but the richness of her early bilingual years gave her much to draw on in her writing.

She is the author of A Tale of Two Migrations a French Canadian Odyssey. Presently, she is working on a memoir entitled Eighty-Five Years of Memory. A Life.

She credits the Women'sWriters Group of South Beach with encouraging her with their enthusiasm and critiques.

She divides her time between Connecticut and The Fountain of Youth.

MARILYN LIEBERMAN

Marilyn Lieberman is a retired college professor, social worker and psychotherapist. For 18 years, she was the Director of the Molloy College social work program. She also held teaching positions at the Rutgers graduate school of social work and Touro College.

Marilyn continues to provide therapy services to her many friends, children, grandchildren, waitresses, car valets, etc. on a pro bono basis. South Beach is Marilyn's second home but her first love. She is thrilled to be part of a community of talented women writers who share a passion for writing and telling stories.

MARJ O'NEILL-BUTLER

Marj O'Neill-Butler, a resident of Miami Beach, Florida, is the Regional Rep for the Dramatists Guild – Florida Region. She is also a member of the New Play Exchange, Honor Roll and the International Center for Women Playwrights. Her work has been seen in 31 states, the District of Columbia, Canada, Great Britain, Scotland, Hong Kong Malaysia, and Seoul, S. Korea. She has had 55 different plays produced in multiple theaters, numerous readings and of course, many rejections. A published playwright and mother of two grown sons, Marj is a proud member of Actors Equity and SAG-AFTRA.

PAMELA REINGOLD MAYER

Pamela Reingold Mayer took her first Miami breath on arrival at Jackson Memorial Hospital. Ms. Mayer's love for all things creative from theatre to art fuels her passion for writing that has led to her originative storytelling. No one and nothing are safe from her looking at the humorous side of life and taking pen to paper. Recently chosen by New Deal Creative Arts in Hyde Park, NY for their You Tube Showcase. Between internet dating and facilitating the Women Writers Group of South Beach she gathers plenty of material. Pamela swears she can write about anything and everything except herself.

ROSA SANTANA

Made in Brazil with Mexican ingredients, Rosa Santana has been writing in her diary since first grade. Her spirited observations made their way into the Miami Herald, The Miami New Times, Enlightened Practice Magazine, the Yogarosa monthly newsletter and blog, and various Yelp reviews.

Investigating impermanence and sorrow in her writing, she sheds hope in the light of Iyengar Yoga, and has faith that mentoring the next generation of teachers will bring peace into the world. Her three daughters were raised on the yogic teachings of non violence and truthfulness. She writes to declutter her mind.

MARY ELLEN SCHERL

After a 15-year career at a Madison Avenue advertising agency, Ms. Scherl transitioned from commercial art to the finer arts of sculpting, painting, installations, photography and most recently writing. Her art is issue based. Body image, cancer, genetics, and our fragile democracy are her narratives. Her writing is about experiences such living in a tent in Alaska for four months, the moments of synchronicity in the journey to find her birth-families, her role as mother of three grown children, her bold adventures and her introspections. She is a Bakehouse Art Complex Resident Artist in Miami. To see her art visit maryellenscherl.com.

IRENE SPERBER

Irene Sperber distinguishes situations using her own peculiar take and word usage. Wry and dry, the observational memoir style glues together verbiage to match the occasion with a mind formed as a visual artist.

Born in Maine, now happily thawed and living in Miami Beach, Sperber has added her brand of critical thinking to years of myriad published art reviews, branching out to turning the mirror on her own art-of-life reexamination.

MIRIAM STEINBERG

Miriam Steinberg is a writer and graphic designer born and bred in Queens, NY. Miriam enjoys spending quality time in Miami Beach where she is thrilled to have insinuated her way into the Women's Writers Group of South Beach.

Long a believer in the adage "truth is stranger than fiction," she writes personal essays and opinion pieces with a healthy dose of irony and humor.

Miriam is most proud of being the oldest graduate in her Creative Writing MFA class, and of her family of course. She looks forward to spending much more quality time in South Florida.

DENA STEWART

New York Teacher, Editor, Corporate Exec.
    Though Dena advanced, pressure made her a wreck.
*"In what profession would you be content
    knowing, most days, that your time was well spent?"*
*"To be a painter as my occupation.
To use art for engagement and education."*
She moved to South Beach, took part in town action,
and founded a nonprofit to lead group interaction.
Dena joined her husband for an online video show
adding to her resume, as newer ventures grow.
Challenges force Dena to reach and to rise.
Her eye is on serenity. *Inner Peace*, the valued prize.

TERRY TRACHT

Terry Tracht was born in Brooklyn, NY, raised on a farm in Vineland, NJ, and spent her teens in her parents' pinball arcade on the Atlantic City Boardwalk. Terry holds a BA in Psychology and Sociology from Douglass College, Rutgers University, a Master of Science in Management from Florida International University and a Juris Doctorate degree from the University of Miami School of Law. She enjoys writing short stories and poetry, and as her favorite subjects are her family members, her work is often laced with humor. Terry loves to travel and has accompanied her husband on several cross country motorcycle trips.

MANDY URENA

Mandy Urena was born in Coventry, England. She is an Air Force wife of 27 years and after training in London, Tokyo and New York, began her massage career as "masseuse to the troops" on military bases in Germany, Spain and Guam. Over a period of almost three decades, she has built an international following including some of the biggest celebrities in the world and people going through cancer. She also worked as an instructor in Philadelphia, teaching a new generation of therapists.

As a world traveler, she has gallivanted through 64 countries and is now settled in Miami Beach, Florida with her husband and their Great Pyrenees, Abraham.

DR. JOYCE ZARITSKY

Dr. Joyce Zaritsky is a retired college professor hatched in the Bronx, New York. She writes to stay out of trouble, although often it results in the opposite. She could easily become the Commissioner of Propaganda for Miami Beach because of her love of this quirky city.

She is a frequent writer of letters to the Miami Herald and other newspapers, has had several pieces published in esoteric literary magazines, has written a novel and is at work on her second. She however, should be well known for the many rejection slips she has framed on the walls of her apartment.

Made in the USA
Columbia, SC
06 July 2022